Peter's Sisters

LM Foster

Copyright © 2016 LM Foster

ISBN-13: 978-0692677247
ISBN-10: 0692677240

Cover Design by
Ravenna Young
www.ravennayoung.blogspot.ca

9th Street Press
www.9thstreetpress.com

When life itself seems lunatic, who knows where madness lies?
Perhaps to be too practical is madness.
To surrender dreams — this may be madness.
Too much sanity may be madness —
and maddest of all: to see life as it is, and not as it should be!

— Miguel de Cervantes, *Don Quixote*

.

Concatenation of a Blended Family
(Shaken Not Stirred), or,
Incest, Southern California Stylie

The group counselor gave us each one of these compact, black and white composition books and suggested that writing down our thoughts and feelings might help us to *get better.* Like I have a sniffle, and some chicken soup and Mommy tucking me in will make it go away. I notice that they do a lot of talking to us like we're children like that here. The place has a lot of pediatric elements to it: the walls are a happy mint green, and there are paintings of non-descript gardens and vases of flowers, absolutely not inviting you to dwell on your problems. There are jigsaw puzzles in the day room, and cartoons or harmless old TV shows or movies playing on the television. When the TV's off, they play the oldies' station on the radio.

There's also no lock on my door, and if I'm not in the dayroom where I can be observed, someone comes by and checks on me every fifteen minutes. Suicide watch, don't you know.

But whatever medication it is that they've got me on – I don't feel suicidal. I never did. That kinda histrionic bullshit was always Bonnie's thing. I just got a little confused. I overreacted, maybe.

I put my name on the inside of the cardboard cover, and my counselor's name, so they can tell my insane ramblings from the next patient's. The counselor said that no one will read what I write unless I offer it to my doctor, however. I'm not sure I'll wanna do that, but since all their *How to Cure the*

Confused manuals have instructed them (and they have instructed me) that writing down my thoughts will make me *get better,* I might as well start at the beginning.

My name is Susan Fisher. I don't have to begin at the very beginning – *I was born,* like David Copperfield – these composition books aren't very thick and the lines are widely spaced. If I start with my birth, I'll fill up a couple of them before I get to where the interesting parts begin.

I'm twenty-five now, but I'll start the story at about thirteen or so, when my parents got divorced. Before someone climbs up on his high horse of *divorce destroys the children, no wonder she's in the nuthouse,* allow me to shoot all that down. There weren't children, there was only child – me – and I enjoyed the certainty that being the only one brings: I always knew that Mommy and Daddy loved me. They just didn't love each other anymore, and apparently hadn't for some time. Their split was quiet, amicable. I actually discovered that my dad did smile sometimes, once he got his own place.

In the middle of my fourteenth year, my mom met a man named Glenn Cox. They dated, and around the time I turned fifteen, they got married. Mom sold the house. It's a sign of just how friendly my parents' divorce had been: she gave a portion of the profits from the sale to Dad.

Glenn's house was bigger. He had two extra rooms upstairs, so Mom and I moved in with him. And also, that way, he didn't have to uproot his son.

Ah, yes, Glenn's son. My new stepbrother. Peter.

Peter was sixteen when our parents married, a little more than a year and a half older than me. For the first four months that we lived under the same roof, we were wary strangers. I knew nothing whatsoever about boys, had never been around any, except at school. I'd never had any for playmates. I wasn't even interested in them yet. So I wasn't at all curious about the silent, alien, redheaded other that was now present at the dinner table every night. I knew that he had lost his mom to leukemia when he was thirteen, and I thought maybe that was why he was so quiet. I thought he probably still missed her.

He was neither sullen nor shy, just watchful. He got along well with my mom, and I got along well with Glenn. Conversation slowly picked up as we all got to know each other and settled into our new life together. Peter went out on the weekends with his friends; if he had a girlfriend, I didn't hear about it. I just wasn't interested in what he was doing. I've always been an introspective dreamer, a reader. And at that time, I was still very much a little girl.

In June, I went away to become the juniorest of counselors at a summer camp in the mountains. Even though you were supposed to be sixteen to be part of the staff, there were three of us that hadn't yet reached that milestone. But they let us in, anyway. They called us *CITs:* Counselors in Training. All of us liked that expression, because it seemed to lessen the responsibility of looking out for the campers somewhat. They were all between eleven and fourteen, not that much younger than us, anyway.

And the older girls, the real counselors, seemed so much older. I'd lived my life up until then through literature, and I thought I knew how things were, because I'd read the timeless words of worldly writers and poets. But these girls were actually living life. There were five of them, two seventeen, two eighteen, and Lois, who was nineteen. I would later reflect that there is not a whole lot of difference between seventeen and nineteen in a young woman's life, but there is a great deal of difference between a sheltered, bookish fifteen and a been-around-the-block seventeen. One might say *a world* of difference.

The campers slept four or five to a cabin; eight cabins in all, two rows of four, separated by a wide expanse of grass. We slept in one big, barracks-like room above the chow hall at the head of the field. The camp director had her own cabin beside the chow hall, so she didn't come upstairs and check on us very often. The rest of the staff, the cooks and the girls in charge of the horses, lived offsite. Camp was a world of girls and women, with not a male to be seen.

Every morning at seven a bell would ring; each counselor would go to her assigned cabin and rouse her campers and bring them up to the chow hall. After breakfast, there were activities, nature hikes and swimming, archery and horseback riding. I was in charge of arts and crafts, and from a big book on the subject, I taught my campers how to do macramé and make pots out of coils of clay. The whole thing was a lot of fun.

But what I remember the most about that summer were the evenings. After dinner, we led sing-alongs, and put on a few skits for the campers, then each counselor listened to problems, mitigated disputes, and tucked her girls in by lights out at eight-thirty, after which we returned to the barracks. Then we were left to our own devices.

Smoking was frowned upon in our area, but it wasn't forbidden, so when one of the older girls offered me a cigarette, I gave it a try. Drugs and drinking were definitely forbidden, but these were modern, American teenage girls, and one night, Lois smuggled in a half a bottle of rum and offered us all a taste, in Dixie cups purloined from the chow hall. Lois trusted us younger girls, was confident that we wouldn't narc her off. All eight of us were in this together, after all. I'd been permitted a glass of champagne at my mother's wedding, so it wasn't my first drink. I got a nice buzz from Lois's warm, iceless rum and Coke.

Deidre produced a joint one Friday evening. This scared my young peers, but I liked Deedee, and I didn't think she'd offer us anything that would harm us. The pot made me feel pleasantly light-headed and surprisingly philosophical, because I became riveted to the conversation that followed. You could say that it opened the doors of perception a little bit for me, for the very first time.

The five older girls started to talk about what they'd left behind for the summer. They agreed that being up there in the mountains amid the clean air and Nature's bounty was swell and all, but they were simpatico on what they missed: the opposite sex. Cellphones were brought out, pictures of current boyfriends and exes were shown. Raunchy stories and explicit descriptions were related, accompanied by gales of stoned giggles. I and my two other virgin confreres listened avidly.

Deidre passed me her phone. "That's Donny. Scroll through. There's a bunch of him on there." She went back to talking to Lois.

The first photo was in black and white, and I blinked at it in surprise and confusion. The smiling young man was my stepbrother, Peter.

I swiped the screen. The next picture was in color, so maybe it was the drugs – I could see that it wasn't Peter at all. It was a selfie of Deedee and her man, and Donny had brown hair, not red, like Peter's, and he was maybe a couple years older. He didn't really resemble my stepbrother at all, once I saw him in color. It wasn't like they could be brothers or anything like that. Cousins, maybe.

I dutifully scrolled through Deidre's many pics of Donny. He was cute, smiling in all of them, definitely unlike Peter, who seldom smiled. He always seemed so serious. I came to another black and white shot – apparently Deidre was a bit of an artistic type – in which Donny was nude.

I'd seen pictures of naked men before – one does not live in the internet age without glimpsing the odd snippet of nudity. Do not, I beseech you, Google *jousting* without the Safe Search on. But always before, I'd just clicked away, because my friends had been there with me, and being little girls, not yet curious, we'd been embarrassed.

But these were my new friends, big girls, and they were definitely not embarrassed by these kinds of things. So I took my time and studied the picture of Deidre's naked boyfriend, standing in a brightly-lit, mirrored bathroom, grinning, ready to go. She happened to be saying to Lois, "He's so proud of the way he looks. He always wants to do it with the lights on." Lois grinned in understanding.

I knew what *it* was, of course, in the strictly clinical sense, the where-babies-come-from sense. The poetic sense. But listening to the older girls' giggling stories and perusing

5

Donny's pictures, I wondered, for the very first time, what it might be like to do these things they were talking about, with someone like him. Just like that, I was interested in boys.

Throughout the rest of the summer, I thought about this thing that men and women did together, this creation of *the beast with two backs.* I asked Deidre questions; she was kind and didn't laugh at my naiveté. My mother had never broached the subject – she'd signed the permission slip in 8th grade so I could learn about human reproduction, and probably figured that was enough, because I'd never asked about it. And one boring, clinical quarter of Sex Ed *had* been enough, right up until I saw that picture of Deidre's naked boyfriend. Now there would be no going back to immature disinterest. Now I was intrigued.

Deedee told me that boys would try to get away with anything I would let them get away with. So if I was interested, I should make them wait before giving in to these still unknown things. "At least three or four dates," she told me, as if I'd ever been on a date. This waiting time would usually secure their loyalty, but not always. Nothing was a sure thing. "You just be careful, Susie," she told me. "Make sure they love you first, before you fall for them."

Glenn and my mom came to pick me up when camp was over. Deedee and I hugged and said goodbye. We were now friends on Facebook, and she promised to keep in touch. But she lived in the next town over from mine, and I wasn't even old enough to drive yet. I was fifteen and a half and never been kissed, and Deidre was a grown woman, at least to me. I didn't think that it was very likely that she'd keep in touch.

On the drive home, I felt like a new arrival from an alien world. There were men everywhere: in the other cars, on the streets, walking around in the mall where we stopped for lunch. Just like there'd always been, of course. Only I'd never noticed them before, and now I contemplated the idea that some of them – the ones my age or a few years older – why, under their clothes, they might look just like Donny, smooth and muscular, ready to go. Suddenly, inexplicably, this idea was inviting to me. I wasn't quite sure how I would proceed if I found myself with a naked guy, but I was definitely sure that I was interested in finding out.

As luck or fate or whatever would have it, there were two half-naked ones sitting in the backyard when we got home. My stepbrother Peter and his friend lounged in lawn chairs, shirtless and barefoot beneath the shade of the big pepper tree. It was Southern-California-in-late-August hot, the dog days, as the saying goes, and they had a sprinkler set up on the walkway, and it alternately watered the grass, arced into the air, then went back the other way and watered *them.* It was a pleasant scene to come home to for someone of my newly discovered interests.

I stopped on the walkway, just to look at them. Glenn had to step around me, and my mom followed him up the back steps and into the house. Peter stared at me for a full thirty seconds, as if he'd never seen me before, and I stared back at him, because it was indeed like I'd never seen *him* before. I was looking at him through new, appreciative eyes.

He smiled. "How was camp?"

"Enlightening," I replied, with what I thought might be an air of mystery.

"You remember Matt?"

I'd never seen his friend in my life, and honestly said, "I can't say as I do." Matt also smiled, rose, shook my hand.

Peter told him my name, referred to me as his sister, and probably just out of politeness, Matt said, "I've heard a lot about you." I doubted it. Why would Peter be mentioning me to his friend? I'd certainly never mentioned him to any of mine.

Matt had a pleasant, attractive face, sandy-colored hair, big brown eyes and a nice smile. But he was chubby, padded with rolls of baby fat. I thought that it probably kept him nice and warm in the winter. I also thought that we'd all be better served if he would put his shirt on.

My stepbrother stood, stretched luxuriantly. I noticed for the first time that he had chiseled – that was really the only word – shoulders and arms; nor was there an ounce of fat on him. The opening lines of *The Fountainhead,* which I'd just read – it had been Lois's – played through my mind. I looked at Peter and saw Howard Roark. *His body leaned back against the sky. It was a body of long straight lines and angles, each curve broken into planes. The wind waved his hair against the sky. His hair was neither blond nor red, but the exact color of ripe orange rind.*

I looked at the outline of his ribs as he arched his back, and my gaze took in those odd muscles that descended from either side of his waist. I had noticed these particularly in Donny's picture, had even Googled what they were called: obliques. It was something I was sure that women also had, but they were somehow startlingly attractive on men. The wet material of Peter's white board shorts molded to the rest of him, and I again thought of that arty black and white photo of Deidre's naked boyfriend.

Peter concluded his stretch, and maybe he noticed where I was looking, because he adjusted the waistband on his shorts so that they hung loosely again. He said to Matt, "Ask Sue what she thinks."

I blinked in surprise. I wasn't quite sure what I was thinking and I surely wouldn't be able to put it into words.

"About what?" Matt asked.

"About *The Blue Lagoon* thing. Get a woman's opinion."

Matt looked down at the ground with what might've been embarrassment for a split-second. "Okay." He met my eyes with an impish smile. "I guess my sister and her boyfriend watched some ancient movie the other night called *The Blue Lagoon.* Netflix was out, something, so they had to look through his mom's old DVDs for something to watch. She told me – it's about these little kids that get shipwrecked on a tropical island. They grow up . . ." He considered Peter for a second, as if for clarification or assistance, but Peter only returned his glance blankly. "They grow up and they fall in love and have a baby and all that. My sister said it was all romantic and stuff."

Matt sat down back down abruptly, looking embarrassed again. Peter fetched another chair and placed it across from theirs, turned off the sprinkler, then quickly got out of the sun. His skin was like milk, like marble. I'd heard his dad say how easily he sunburned.

He smiled at me again, and I noticed that his eyes were a pale, jade green. I thought it peculiar that I'd never noticed the color of my stepbrother's eyes before, nor that they twinkled. He said, "I think that's all bullshit."

It was obvious that some response was expected of me. "What's all bullshit?"

"This love story. *The Blue Lagoon.* Two little kids, growing up by themselves. They wouldn't know how to . . ." He grinned crookedly at his friend. "I supposed they kissed?"

Matt shrugged. "I guess. I didn't see it. But . . . yeah. They did everything. Cathy said the girl wound up having a baby."

Peter turned his smile upon me again. It was so strange to see him smile. He had very nice teeth, and I remembered a shot of him from some album of his family that Mom had showed me – a grinning redheaded boy with braces. He was surely a boy no longer.

"And I'm saying it's all bullshit. Two little kids, without any adults around . . . Kissing and sex . . . I'm saying, that's all learned behavior. They'd never figure it out on their own. Someone has to teach you how to kiss, someone that's seen it before, like in the movies, or seen other people doing it. And you hear about sex, or you see it online . . ." I thought his green eyes darkened a shade as he held my gaze. "They'd just be like any other brother and sister that grew up together. They wouldn't want to . . . They'd never figure it out on their own."

"Sure they would, Pete," Matt said. I broke my stepbrother's lingering stare and gave his friend my attention. "It's a natural, physical function. You get to a certain age, the hormones start . . . They might not know *why* they wanted to do it . . . I don't know about the *feelings,* but they would want to . . . It's just natural. No one would have to teach them."

9

"You have to see other people kiss," Peter insisted. "That's a cultural thing. Don't they say that Eskimos don't kiss? What do you think, Sue?"

"I don't know anything about Eskimos," I said. Nor did I know anything about kissing, except, as Peter had said, what I'd seen couples do on the street and in the movies. Just like everything else about the opposite sex, I'd never before given it much consideration. But he didn't know anything about my lack of experience, and the thought that now followed was: How much does he and even chubby Matt know about kissing?

They waited for my opinion, and I found that I didn't have to consider too long to give it to them. My own recent *awakening* – how's that for a poetic word? That in itself demonstrated that Peter was wrong. Hadn't I suddenly become curious about boys after seeing a picture of one of them naked? If this guy was running around naked on a tropical island, wouldn't the girl become curious one day, too?

"I agree with Matt. It would all just come naturally." Finding out about these things seemed like the most natural thing in the world to me right then. "Nobody has to teach animals. And aren't we just–"

"Man is a cultural animal," Peter said. "We have to be taught right from wrong, who and when–"

"But if there wasn't anyone there to teach them all that, they'd still figure out the basics on their own," Matt argued.

"I dunno," Peter said. He still stared at me. Then my phone beeped and I looked away from him.

R u home yet? my friend Stacy texted. *Can I come c u?*

Yes & yes, I texted back. *I've missed u! Come over right now!*

When I'd left for camp in June, Stacy had been a little girl, just like I was. I wondered what she'd been doing all summer. Had she grown up like me? I couldn't wait to discuss all these new things I'd discovered with her.

Matt and Peter and I talked about the school year that would be coming up in a few weeks, and made other small talk about the hot weather, and short, nothing comments about the latest clips going viral on the internet. I watched Peter with an entirely new awareness when he stood and rubbed sunscreen on his muscled arms, across his smooth, hairless chest, his flat belly, his sculpted obliques. I was just thinking that it would be the sisterly thing to do to offer to get his back for him, when Stacy's mom dropped her off in the alley behind the house.

She paused at the gate, squealed, and ran up the walkway. I barely had time to stand before she gave me a big squeeze. "I missed you so much!"

Stacy glanced at our companions, then her eyes flickered back to me. From the unexpectedly *hungry* look on her face, I could tell that she'd experienced an awakening of her own sometime this summer.

"This is my brother Peter and his friend Matt." They stood, shook Stacy's hand. There was some *learned behavior,* I thought, something we'd all been taught to do. Even Eskimos shake hands.

Peter fetched another chair, and the four of us sat in silence and stared at each other for the span of probably a good minute. Then Matt said, "What would you ladies like to do this afternoon?"

Stacy stole a glance at me and I got the impression that *doing something with boys* was perhaps not quite as novel an idea to her as it was to me. What had she been up to all summer?

Peter scrolled on his phone. "The new *Superman's* showing in an hour. You guy's wanna go see that?"

Stacy's winningest smile surprised me. "That sounds great!"

Peter also seemed a mite taken aback by her enthusiasm and didn't comment. Instead, he said to Matt, "Sound good?" Matt nodded and smiled at me, and his smile was almost as bright as Stacy's.

They went inside to change; Stacy and I watched them go. I opened my mouth to regale her with all the new things I'd been thinking about, but she beat me to it.

"I kissed Kevin Andrews!" she gushed.

11

"Who?"

"Kevin Andrews. It was at the Fourth of July barbeque. He's my cousin's friend. It was . . . it was great!"

Great was Stacy's go-to adjective. The weather was *great,* - going to the movies with Peter and Matt promised to be *great,* kissing Kevin Andrews had been *great.* I waited for a more in-depth description.

"We were tossing a Frisbee and it went behind the garage. I went to get it, and he followed me. I turned around, and he kinda pushed me up against the garage and kissed me. I . . . I was surprised. I liked it very much."

I found her report disappointing. "Did he . . . did he do anything else?"

"He tried to grab my boob, but I pushed his hand away. So he just kissed me some more, and I . . . kissed him back."

This seemed to be the extent of her tale, but on the other hand, the Fourth of July had passed some time ago, so maybe, since then . . . "Have you . . .?"

Stacy shook her head. "He lives in Orange County, and he was only in town for the weekend. But we spent every second we could together."

"Kissing?"

She nodded, smiled in glee. "I haven't seen him since, but we text. He says as soon as he gets his driver's license, he'll come up and see me."

So Kevin was another of the non-mobile, like Stacy and myself. Before I could ask for further details, the not-non-mobile reappeared in the back doorway. Since they didn't gesture for us to follow them into the house to the front where Peter's car was parked, it was apparent that Matt was going to drive. His car was in the alley by the back gate.

As they walked on ahead of us toward the car, Stacy whispered, closely into my ear, "Your brother's cute."

Was he? I looked at him. He didn't seem to be so much anymore, now that he was dressed. But I had to admit, when I'd seen him sitting there shirtless . . . I'd definitely been put in

12

mind of his resemblance to Deedee's boyfriend. And Donny certainly was cute.

The movie was *meh,* as I find all cinema from the Marvel Comics world to be. Matt sat on one side of me, and Stacy on the other, with Peter next to her. She didn't talk to me, however: she spent the entire time leaned over close to my stepbrother – he that she found so *cute.* I scootched forward once and looked over at him; he only smiled back blankly. Whatever. I didn't really have too much time to think about what they were doing, because Matt had decided that he wanted to hold my hand, and I decided that it was nice.

On the drive home, I noticed that Stacy sat very close to Peter in the back seat, but anytime I peeped over my shoulder at them, he just gave me that same blank smile. It was still so odd to see him smile. He seemed to be mostly ignoring Stacy's happy chatter, her insistent proximity to him.

These double dates, if you will, continued for the rest of the summer, and on the weekends after school started. Matt continued to hold my hand, and put his arm around me. When we went to the movies alone one time, he kissed me, and just like Stacy had said, it was *great.* I liked it very much.

But also like Stacy, when he tried to put his hands on me, I pushed them away. Kissing was all right, but I wasn't ready for anything else yet. Matt was nice and all, but he was chubby, and thinking about what I'd seen of him without his shirt on didn't elicit any desire in me to touch him, so I surely didn't want him touching me. But kissing him was definitely all right.

Stacy was having no such luck with Peter. She told me that he would also hold her hand and occasionally put his arm around her shoulders, but no kissing had not been forthwith.

"Why don't you just kiss *him?"* I asked.

"I dunno, Sue. Somehow, I just don't think I could . . . Although, it does seem like he's waiting for . . . *something.* But . . . I just couldn't go on ahead and kiss him. Maybe he'd turn me down. Maybe he's not interested. Maybe he doesn't like me." Then she pouted and sent a text to Kevin, still marooned behind the Orange Curtain without transportation. He was as

13

far away from Stacy and her desire to be kissed as were the young lovers in *The Blue Lagoon* away from civilization.

"Ask your brother if he likes me, Sue," Stacy requested, after another movie date passed without any overtures. "I wanna know if I'm wasting my time."

I thought it was strange that Peter hadn't taken the bait. He seemed to like her; they laughed and joked, texted and talked on the phone together, just like Matt and I did. To an outside observer, it would seem that we were two happy adolescent couples. But all was not well; I wasn't at all inclined to progress any further with Matt, and Peter didn't even want to kiss Stacy.

So when Matt dropped us off at home after our date that Friday, I aimed to do just what my friend had requested, and ask Peter what he thought of her. Our parents weren't home – it was their own date night – and sometime later, I would remember Kipling's words from *Great Expectations,* which we were just then covering in English: *Pause you who read this, and think for a moment of the long chain of iron or gold, of thorns or flowers, that would never have bound you, but for the formation of the first link on one memorable day.*

The second floor of Glenn's house was comprised of a small landing/hall area and two fair-sized bedrooms. Then there was a bathroom and another tiny bedroom, used for storage, beside that. The two big bedrooms (Peter's and mine) were connected by a large, walk-through closet, crammed full of the stuff he had accumulated in his sixteen years on his side, and the stuff I'd moved in, on my side. It wasn't as if we could actually walk through it. Not then, anyway.

I went upstairs first – he remained in the kitchen, to make himself a snack, I think. I wiped off my make-up, and changed out of my date clothes. I'd really never been much for getting dressed up, but Stacy always insisted that *we look our best* for our *dates.* When I heard the muffled gunfire from one of Peter's video games in the next room, I decided that the time was nigh to ask my friend's question.

I knocked on his door; the noise ceased immediately. After a slight pause, he told me to come in.

I'd never been in Peter's room before, nor he mine, since Mom and I had come to live there. I was surprised at how similarly they were set up. Just like me, Peter had a television on the wall, beside the closet door, and his bed was against the opposite wall, facing it. Beside his bed was a bookshelf, messy, haphazardly crammed to overflowing with scores of paperbacks, just like in my room. There was a night stand with a lamp – the lamp was the other half of a pair to the one I read by at night.

He reached over and switched the light on, the game controller still in his other hand. I discovered that he was again shirtless, wearing only another pair of board shorts, and the whiteness of his skin was stark in contrast to the dark green of his sheets. I thought without really thinking that the color complimented his eyes. He scootched up until he was sitting with his back against the headboard. He crossed his ankles and looked expectantly at me. He didn't speak.

I got right to the point. He was supposed to be my brother, was he not, in name if not in blood or history? Weren't we friends? "You know, Stacy's my best friend. We talk."

He had no response to that.

"She wants to know if you like her. She wants to know why you haven't–"

"Done what you and Matt do?"

"How do you know what Matt and I do?"

"We talk, too." Peter swung his long legs over the side of the bed and gestured for me to sit beside him.

"We haven't done anything except–"

"Make out a little bit." Peter smiled slyly, just for a second. "I know. He told me. He's says you're a tiresomely good girl, always slapping his hands away. So I could ask you the same question. Why haven't you and Matt . . . Are you afraid?"

I sighed and sat down beside him. "I dunno, Pete. I don't think I'm afraid. I'm just not . . ."

15

"You're just not into him?"

It was one of those expressions you hear in the movies all the time, a cliché, really. But it was true, nonetheless. I just wasn't into Matt. He was nice and all, polite, pleasant, but he just wasn't attractive to me. Kissing him was all right, but all the things that I thought that I might want to do with someone that looked like Donny . . . I just couldn't quite picture doing them with chubby Matt.

"He's not your type." A statement from Peter, and it was right on the mark, even if it was another cliché. "And Stacy – she's not really my type, either."

I was again remembering that black and white photo of Deedee's boyfriend, long and lean, so I really wasn't giving my full attention to Peter when he said, "I thought there was something different about you when you came back from camp. The way you looked at me . . ."

Peter put his hand on my cheek and kissed me then, slowly, and before I quite knew what I was doing, I was kissing him back, because *oh, God!* Suddenly, here was the electricity I'd always dreamed about, the thrumming of the blood in my ears, the dark urgency to do I wasn't quite sure what. Kissing Matt was nice, but kissing pale, green-eyed, long and lean Peter! I pulled him closer to me, kissed him harder. This must be what it would be like to kiss Donny! Peter! My . . . stepbrother . . .

He must've thought the same thing because he broke the kiss, looked down at the floor. "But we're . . ." He kissed me again, stopped.

"We're not really . . ." I kissed him this time, the thing Stacy had been afraid to do. But I wasn't afraid.

He stopped again, stared at me. His hand, still on my cheek, was firm and damp. His eyes were a darker green now, depthless in their confused hesitance. Then he assumed a measure of control. "We shouldn't do this, Sue."

But I was still lost in the thrill of the moment, the *naturalness of it*. This was how those kids on that island would've felt, and I reveled in it, as if I was like them, as if I also hadn't had any *learned behavior,* no concept *of right and wrong,* of *who and when.*

This is how it *should* feel to be kissed. Peter wasn't really my brother, now was he? I'd only known him for six or seven months. Just because our parents were man and wife, just because we'd assumed these artificial roles as siblings, didn't mean . . .

I wanted to feel his mouth on mine again, wanted him to touch me like Matt wanted to touch me. I wanted to touch him like Stacy longed to do. There was nothing wrong with it; it was the most natural thing in the world. But I saw it in his eyes: *My dad, your mom – what would they think? People at school . . .*

"It'll be our secret," I said. Another cliché. I tried to kiss him again.

"It'll have to be, Sue," he warned me. "No one can find out about this. It's—"

"It's not wrong, Pete." To prove it wasn't, I kissed him again.

He pushed me gently away, but not too far. "But it's not right, either. We can never be . . . together, in public. Like boyfriend and girlfriend."

Never was a long time, I thought. But he was right. We couldn't be boyfriend and girlfriend *now.* We were supposed to be brother and sister.

"And someday, there'll be other people . . ." His expression wanted me to agree with this. Other Stacys and other Matts, others, someday, maybe more to our *type,* but not designated by the whim of our parents' marriage as brothers and sisters.

I thought that *someday* was as far away and as inconsequential as *never,* so I again said, "It'll be our secret."

"Pinkie swear." Peter smiled, and crooked his long, white baby finger at me. "We promise to never tell another living soul about this."

It seemed a trifle girlish to me, but I guess the right and wrong of it was weighing on him. It was the first time in my

17

life that I'd ever *wanted* something so utterly – I would've agreed to sell my soul to Satan right then, if only he'd just kiss me again.

In retrospect, maybe I did.

I remembered Stacy's words then. *It does seem like he's waiting for . . . something.* And like a divine revelation, a Jovian thunderbolt from on high, I realized what it was. Peter had been waiting for *me*.

I crooked my finger around his, told him I swore that I'd never tell.

And I never have, until now. And this isn't really telling. I can always destroy this composition book. It's all just an exercise to help me *get better,* is it not? The shrinks don't even want to read it, unless I give it to them. And Peter and me – that has nothing whatsoever to do with why I'm here. I only mention it because I might as well start at the beginning.

Even though you could say that I was like the girl, I discovered that Peter was not at all like the innocent boy on the tropical island in that movie, the-never-to-this-day-viddied *Blue Lagoon.* His own summer of awakening had obviously already occurred, because Peter had more than a handful of condoms in his bedside table, and within a week, he'd made me an appointment at Planned Parenthood. He waited in the car while I went in and got a prescription for birth control pills. There would be no surprise babies on our secret isle.

I don't know about *better,* but reminiscing about Peter has definitely made me feel warm and fuzzy. Thinking about him – It's *great,* just like Stacy used to say. I think I'll go take a shower. I have to make it quick, though. They come looking for me if I'm gone for more than fifteen minutes.

BONNIE'S JOURNAL, PART ONE

I visited Susan at the home today.

That's the nice word for it. *Funny Farm, Nuthouse, Loony Bin.* Those are all the terms Dad uses. He thinks it's all a big joke, says it was just a little *spring fever,* a little bit of jealousy, that led Susan to do and say what she did. "The best cure for a man is another man, Bonnie," he said. "Susie just thought she'd take yours." Ha ha.

I don't see one thing funny about that, Dad. Not one thing.

"She'll get over it, honey. She'll realize her mistakes. She's just confused right now."

Susan had one of those old-fashioned Composition Books, like they gave you in grade school, on the table next to her bed. I politely asked her what it was and reached for it, but she snatched it away and stuck it under her pillow. She said the doctors had told her to write down her feelings, that it was supposed to help her with her therapy. She said what was in there was none of my business.

Like I want to read her insane ramblings, anyway.

But maybe that's not fair. I love Sue. She's my sister, after all, and she helped me through my own rough patch some time back. But this rudeness – not to mention what she tried to do to Jay, what she said about him – it's making it hard to keep on loving her.

My friends are divided – forgive her, she had a breakdown; or, ghost her, she's nuts. Jay himself says that the decision is up to me, whether I want to keep her in my life. For his own part, he says, he'll never turn his back on her again.

My friend Mona says maybe I should consider therapy myself. She's says it's not an easy thing to get over on your own, when your sister wigs out. When she claims all kinds of lies about your boyfriend. Mona says it couldn't hurt to talk about it to a neutral, third party.

But the whole thing is just too sordid, too ridiculous. Susan had a breakdown – I had one myself, once. I don't need to drag in a neutral third party to listen to my troubles.

But seeing Susan's Composition Book gave me an idea. Maybe it would help to talk to *myself* about it. Hence this file. BONNIE'S JOURNAL, PARTS ONE THROUGH INFINITY! But I'm surely not gonna write mine out longhand, like poor Sue has to do. I can type mine, unlike her. I understand they don't let them have phones or computers at the home.

Where should I start? I guess the best place to begin would be how I came to meet Susan, how she came to become my sister. I'll tell it like I was telling it to a stranger. Maybe she did what she did because there *are* some kind of unresolved issues that I've never considered, and maybe I'll see them. Maybe they'll come out in the telling.

My mom and dad divorced when I was a child. Mom was a career gal, and her career took her out of town a lot. I don't remember her all that well. She calls on my birthday, and sends a check at Christmas, but if I'm truthful, she's really just a voice on the other end of the phone. They divorced when I was five, Dad got custody, and Mom moved away to pursue her career. Something in the banking biz.

I've had a succession of other mommies throughout my life. They were all nice and kind to me, but none of them lasted for very long. Some for a few months or a few weeks or sometimes just a long weekend. I never had time to think of any of them as mommies, really, or of their kids as brothers and sisters. They were just Dad's friends, fleeting, impermanent.

My dad's gypsy love life at last came to an end when I was twenty. That's when he met, fell in love with, and married a widow named Vanessa. Just like my previous short-term moms, Vanessa was nice to me. Dad and I gave up our apartment and moved into her big house with her daughter and son. It looked as though I'd have a family at last.

My new brother and sister – that was Susan and Peter. I'll get to Peter and what a son of a bitch he is in a minute, but first, I should talk about Sue. How much she's always meant to me.

She was twenty-two when our parents married. She was working at an office downtown, but still lived at home. She said she longed to be free, but her stepfather had died suddenly just over a year before Vanessa and Dad met, and she'd wanted to stay close to her mom after that, to look after her. Susan confided in me that she was glad that her mom and my dad had fallen in love and married. She admitted that it had been quick, but on the other hand she was thankful – it wasn't like her stepfather was ever coming back.

Susan and I hit it off immediately. I'd always wanted a sister, someone to confide in, someone whom I could trust with my silly thoughts and ideas. I'd always been a loner, and except for Mona, hadn't had too many friends. Now I finally had a close one living right there across the hall from me.

We were so happy to have each other; the suddenness of it made us giddy, like little girls. We giggled and shared clothes and make-up and jewelry, like we were still in high school. I'll never understand why Susan opted not to go to college. I think she's brilliant. Mom, from Atlanta or Chicago or New York or wherever she's living these days, is paying my way through school, and my new sister helped me with all my English classes. I used to think that maybe some kind of teaching thing might be my major if I could ever made up my mind to pick one, but I'm not so sure about the teaching thing now, because sometimes the discussions in English still go right over my head. But back then, Susan always understood, and I was glad for her explanations.

We talked about men. She was dating some guy named George at the time, but she said it wasn't anything serious. She said George was another reason why she'd been hesitant to move out of her mom's house. She thought that George would've wanted to move in with her, or at least he would've wanted to be there all the time. And while Sue claimed to like him, she said she certainly didn't love him, and surely wouldn't have wanted him around all the time.

She mentioned that she'd once talked about going in halfsies with her brother on a place. But then his dad had passed, and he was sad, and both of them decided to stay at home with Vanessa.

As things would turn out, I wish that Peter *had* moved out, that I'd never even met him

.

Incest, Part Two, or Another Family Blended

Angela cried in group today. She sobbed, she bawled, she boo-hooed. When her husband left her, she said that she just couldn't see the point of continuing with life. She still can't see the point, and that's why she's here, why someone checks in on her every fifteen minutes, to make sure she *is* going on. Working through her sadness. *Getting better.*

Bonnie stopped by to see me after school. I didn't know she was coming, and surely hadn't expected her, so my notebook was right out there in the open. Yeah, that wouldn't do at all, to have Bonnie find out about Peter and me, after all this time. Yikes! She surely wouldn't come to visit me any more if she found out about all that. She might even talk that bastard Jay into pressing charges. But if he does, then I will, too . . . Actually, I've wondered why there haven't been any detectives in here to interview me about what happened yet. Maybe they're waiting for me to *get better* first. Maybe they figure a hysterical mental patient makes a bad witness. But my story isn't gonna change.

Ah, Bonnie. My delicate, naïve, unstable, stupid stepsister. Just like Bugs Bunny said in the cartoon playing in the day room this morning: *What a maroon!* I'm tired of looking out for her. She never listens to my advice anyway. She's still devoted to that conniving thief. I'm done trying to protect her.

I'm sure that my as-yet-unseen doctor would want me to write down my feelings about Bonnie, however. After all, it was my efforts to show her how deluded she is in her high opinion of Jay that landed me here in the first place.

Before I get to Bonnie, however, I should finish up about Peter and me, all the better to segue into her chapter.

My stepbrother and I carried on our thing throughout high school, throughout his college career and my start in the workaday world. We carried on our thing right up until he moved to the beach – it always strikes me as hilarious that white-skinned, redheaded, easily sunburned Peter wound up living at that beach. We've spent a few weekends together since he left town. But for the last year or so, Peter's been living with some chick, and I've been somewhat caught up in trying to save Bonnie from herself. I haven't seen him at all lately. I miss him.

Peter and I never got caught. Never even came close to getting caught, never even entered the zip code of Getting Caught, USA, population, us. To mom and Glenn, we were just an amicable brother and sister. They never even suspected the things that their children got up to late at night sometimes, just upstairs.

Why should they? They never ventured up to our part of the house. They were forward thinking parents, believing that we, as nearly adults, had a right to our privacy. In high school, they housed us, fed us, gave us funds, but it wasn't like Mom was up there cleaning our rooms, or Glenn was up there having heart-to-hearts with his son. We were expected to clean our own rooms, do our own laundry, fix ourselves something to eat if we were hungry and not make a mess with it. And we loved these responsibilities, because taking care of them demonstrated our maturity, and it kept Mom and Dad out of our hair.

And of course, as had been prophesied, Peter and I dated other people. By the time he was nineteen and I eighteen, it was even tacitly agreed that we were allowed to stay out overnight with our dates without any parental repercussions, as long as we were considerate enough to check in so they didn't worry about us. We were legally adults by then, after all.

But neither Peter nor I ever snuck any of our belles or beaux up to our rooms. The second floor was reserved for us and our secrets. When we started dating someone new, there was a nod to monogamy and loyalty and all that good stuff for a few days or a week or a month. But that never lasted, and we rationalized the treachery away with the idea that it was our own little thing, our secret. It wasn't really like cheating on them because it had existed before them, and it would continue to exist after they had moved on, as they always did. Neither of us had any relationships that ever lasted.

It wasn't like Peter and I discussed the future; it was a kind of implicit understanding that we had. I think that there was an idea in the background that someday one of us would meet someone, and that person would be the one for us, and then we would remain loyal to that person, and our secret would then come to an end. But in the meantime, during the search, what they would never know about could never possibly hurt them.

A complete trust existed between Peter and me. We knew each other, inside and out. We were cut from the same cloth, as the old saying goes. Like me, he was literate. One of our greatest amusements was the eternal question: "Hey, did you ever read . . .?" It was always fun to share our thoughts on some classic old novel, always a delight to read Shakespeare together. On that score, he was unlike anyone I've ever known, and I was different than all the girls he knew, their lives lived on Facebook, the entirety of their wit summable in 140 Twitter characters. Peter and I were a rarity in the modern world, both readers-for-pleasure, except when we were something else for each other's pleasure. We were copasetic.

We didn't have to play the tiresome games inherent in new relationships, didn't have to jump through any hoops to prove our worth. No unusual or subtle signals had to be deciphered. All that was necessary was a glance or a certain tilt to the head, a texted *Come, shall we about it?* and after our parents retired for the night, we wordlessly comforted each other through the break-ups and the frustrations, and sometimes just for the sure satisfaction of a familiar partner who was always impressed with you, without you even having to try.

25

At twenty-three, Peter graduated from college with a degree in some kind of engineering. Civil, I think it is. I never followed his ambitions that closely. He wasn't my boyfriend, after all; it wasn't necessary for me to praise his scholastic accomplishments and build up his competitive ego. He had Sandy and Helen and Francie for all that. When they let him down, in one way or another, as they always did, I built up his ego in other areas.

I think that another great aspect of our thing was the complete lack of a social element to it. One talks about one's boyfriends and husbands to one's friends and co-workers. One praises and is proud, or alternately, one bitches and complains. Jerry just got a promotion, we're gonna buy a new car; or Eddie is a slob, he always leaves his dirty socks on the bathroom floor. I sometimes thought that the entire point of having girlfriends was the satisfaction of the idea that, yeah, my ol' man might not be Prince Charming, but I'd never put up with the shit she puts up with.

It's just the way things work; we put out the story of our romantic situations, and our friends judge it, then we react to their judgments. We become smug if we have a loyal, hard-working, socially acceptable man, or we become resentful if he's a lazy, drunken bum. Our original assessment of him – he must've been okay in the beginning, because we picked him, didn't we? – is slowly replaced in our mind by our friends' estimation of him.

But all this was absent from my relationship with Peter. The raised eyebrows and shaken heads that would've resulted from the news that I was involved with my stepbrother, and had been so since we were teenagers: non-existent. Why was it that he was often quiet, ruminative, or, alternately, caustic and sarcastic? Why wasn't he outgoing, the life of the party, like Carrie's boyfriend? None of these thoughts ever crossed my mind, because I never heard anyone else's thoughts on Peter. I liked him just the way he was, and never had any cause to doubt my opinion of him, based on the opinions of others.

Then Peter was working and I was working and we briefly discussed the idea of taking our bizarre, unnatural, secretive show on the road, of getting ourselves a two bedroom apartment somewhere, a place to which we probably wouldn't have brought our dates, any more than we'd brought them to our parents' house. Or, maybe that would've changed. Maybe an apartment wouldn't have remained our own secret space like the second floor was. Maybe we would've found those others, maybe they would've become significant, and maybe our thing would've ceased. I dunno. We never got the chance to find out, because in the space of a short year, three rather life-changing events occurred.

The first was tragic. At just fifty-five, Glenn had a heart attack and passed away. My mom was devastated. Unlike her forgotten relationship with my dad, the one that had produced me, Mom's marriage to Glenn had been full of love and friendship. I had cared for him, too. He was a good man. Peter and I tried to comfort Mom as much as we could, but the support of her children, grieving themselves, wasn't a lot of help.

And Peter grieved keenly. He liked my mom, of course, but he considered himself an orphan now, alone, adrift. He was despondent. He dumped whatever Barbie or Cindy he was going with at the time, and I would lie beside him in his narrow bed at night and hold him while he cried. He grimly arose and went to work every day, and eventually this helped the grief to pass. His father's ghost saved him on that score: Peter knew that Glenn wouldn't've wanted him to abandon what he'd worked so hard for in school. Glenn wouldn't have wanted Peter to give up his new career and wallow in self-pity.

The second event that occurred, just after the anniversary of Glenn's passing, was that Mom met John Putman. Their courtship was whirlwind, the marriage quick. Unable to throw off an uncharacteristic bit of childishness, a momentary feeling that his father had been forgotten by his widow, Peter murmured, *"The funeral baked meats did coldly furnish forth the marriage tables."*

But his pique was short-lived, because Peter is nothing if not a realist. He knew in his heart that Mom had loved his father and would never forget him. But there was no call to go on mourning forever. We were both glad that she'd been fortunate enough to again find someone.

And the third occurrence: into our lives did John Putman bring his darling daughter, Bonnie. She was twenty, a frizzy, blonde-haired, blue-eyed ray of sunshine. She didn't even mind being shoved into the tiny bedroom across the hall from ours. The Christmas decorations and old computers, broken televisions and the odd stepladder were now consigned to the garage, and bonny Bonnie moved right on in to the postage stamp-sized space with a smile on her dimpled face.

You'd think that her presence on the same floor would've put a crimp in my incestuous activities with Peter, but there was that closet that separated our rooms. I think it suddenly added a new element of spice to it for him, this idea that the interloper across the hall might at any moment catch wise to what was going on between her new stepbrother and stepsister. It surely brought him out of his depression, and we had a lot of silent giggles together when he would slowly open the closet door and peep around it theatrically in the middle of the night. I would of course know he was coming. We had long ago worked out a flawlessly innocent-seeming text language. Cellphones fallen into the wrong hands would've revealed nothing.

Bonnie developed a crush on Peter from the very beginning. She felt no shame, no need to try to disguise it. She saw no artificial sibling appearances to be kept up. Peter wasn't even remotely her brother: he was her dad's wife's stepson. Peter was blood to no one in the house. Besides, Bonnie considered herself an adult. No one would look askance at her attraction to him.

I watched Peter consider it. A barely raised eyebrow asked my opinion; an almost imperceptible shrug on my part told him to go for it. What did I care? Bonnie was no different from any of the other girls he'd dated in the past, and in the real world, I was seeing big George from Accounting those days, anyway.

I learned that there was soon a succinct discussion between John and his wife's second husband's orphaned son, however. John didn't care if Peter dated his daughter, but he wasn't going to put up with any hanky-panky going on between them under his roof. It just wouldn't be . . . *seemly.*

I laughed at Peter, called him Cinderella, told him that his new wicked stepsister and her affection for him were gonna get him kicked out into the cold. "And without your having attended a single Ball!" Then I added, "What's not *seemly,* is that you'd get to have two women. Right across the hall from each other."

He shrugged. "You get to have two men."

"Indeed I do," I said, and kissed him on the nose. "But George is beginning to bore me, and I think the gig is up with you and Bonnie, before it even begins. There's no closet between your rooms, and John'll be watching. What are you gonna do?"

Peter smiled slyly. "I don't have to do anything. You haven't noticed that our Bonnie's got an attitude? Daddy's not gonna tell her how to live her life. Why, she's practically twenty-one. She's decided to move out, to get her own place. Her mom's gonna pay for it."

So, before Bonnie had even completely unpacked all of her cutely decorated cardboard boxes, she repacked them again. She cashed the check her mom sent to cover the first, last, and security deposit, and she rented herself a tiny apartment downtown. She even got an after-school job waiting tables at some dive called *Mickey's,* for walking-around money. All so she could be free to entertain our stepbrother of an evening. Peter was just that cute to her.

The object of Bonnie's rather single-minded devotion continued to reside in the home in which he'd grown up, however. John knew that on the nights that Peter wasn't there for dinner, he was undoubtedly overnighting with Bonnie, but it didn't seem to bother the old man too much. His daughter was twenty-one now, an actual adult, and what wasn't going on under his roof – why, he didn't have any control over that, now did he?

I thought that my mother might've lost another husband, another coronary would've ensued, if John had found out what his daughter's beloved boyfriend and his stepdaughter were doing under his roof on the nights that Peter *was* home. It wasn't hardly seemly. The thought of the look on his face had he known amused me a great deal, because I didn't care for John the way I had for my first stepfather. John always seemed like a controlling blowhard to me. Yet he made my mom happy, so he couldn't be all bad.

And Peter certainly made Bonnie happy. She was deliriously, giddily, childishly in love with our aloof, secretive, completely grown-up stepbrother. I listened to her delighted tales of his wonderfulness: how sweet and thoughtful he was, how he sometimes surprised her with flowers or candy or a candlelit dinner. Oh, how attentive was Peter!

I remembered how thoughtful and attentive and boyfriend-like he'd been with Stacy, too, whom he hadn't even bothered to kiss. That not-relationship had only lasted until Kevin from Orange County had acquired the means to visit Stacy. Peter's thoughtfulness had been immediately forgotten once a real boyfriend arrived on the scene, one that had been willing to kiss her and touch her. Matt had also moved on to more accessible pastures, about the same time. Stacy and I drifted apart. I haven't talked to her in years.

It wasn't like Peter was unresponsive to Bonnie, as he'd been to Stacy when we were teenagers. I got to hear all the intimate details of how wonderful Peter was on the physical plane also, stuff I knew about far more familiarly than Bonnie could've even dreamed. Yet from her tales, I learned that Peter didn't let all of his cats and kitties out of the bag for her; it seemed that he reserved some of his splendid tricks just for me.

But still did Bonnie love him, and her constant, gushing reiteration of *how much she loved Peter,* made me stop and think. Did I love him? Did he love me? Had either of us ever loved anyone? In a world of red roses and pink hearts, yellow stars and green clovers, of the possibility of thrilling emotions to the height and depth and breadth our souls could reach, had Peter and I really ever been anything other than opportunists? Trying out this one and that one, searching for our type, but always returning to each other, in secret?

You couldn't really call that love, could you? Peter and I had *a thing;* we valued each other. I guess you could even say we needed each other. But the silly happiness that Bonnie encompassed at the very mention of his name? I certainly didn't feel that way about him, and I was sure that he certainly didn't feel that way about her.

And then came the evening when Bonnie called me after her shift at the bar and quietly asked me if I'd seen Peter over the last couple of days. I had not; I'd assumed he'd been with her.

"It's not my week to watch him, Bonnie," I told her. "If he wasn't at your place, I'm sure he was home." He could've been. I didn't keep that close of tabs on him.

He was home now. I was sitting in his room with him. He paused his game and looked intently at me, waiting.

"I think he's cheating on me, Susan!" she wailed.

I looked at Peter curiously. "Why would you think that, honey?"

Peter gave me a *What?* face, so I clicked my phone onto speaker.

"He hasn't stayed here for three days! He says he's tired, some big project at work–"

"I'm sure that's what it is then, Bonnie. I'm sure Peter would never–"

"I had lunch with him today. He was taking me back to school, and some guy cut him off. He had to stomp on the brakes. A tube of lipstick rolled out from under the seat. I picked it up. He didn't see me . . ."

Peter's adorable ginger eyebrows rose. This was all news to him.

"That's not hardly a sex tape, Bonnie," I told her. I'd tried to talk him into that once, when I was in a playful mood. But Peter knew better. Such a thing was *evidence,* and could only be used against him.

I said to my stepsister, "It's probably my lipstick."

"How many lipsticks do you have?" she again wailed. "Two?"

She was right. I wasn't really into wearing make-up. I didn't even wear lipstick to work.

"It's not your shade, anyway. He had another girl in his car! He's cheating on me, Sue!"

"I'm sure you're just overreacting," I said, trying to calm her down. She was positively frantic. "Maybe he gave some girl from work a ride home or something. I'm sure he's not–"

"Oh, my God, Sue! What am I gonna do?"

Scream and cry at him, dump him. Or just let it ride. How the hell should I know? I'd never suspected any of them of cheating on me, because I just hadn't cared enough to worry about it. I had cheated on all of them, after a fashion, had I not, so what difference did it really make what they did? I looked at my stepbrother for suggestions as to what I should say to his hysterical girlfriend, but he just shrugged.

"Why don't you just call him? Ask whose lipstick it is?"

"That would make it sound like I suspect him."

"But you do suspect him, Bonnie!" *And you're probably right,* I thought. That lipstick had to belong to somebody.

"I have to find out for sure," she whispered. "And then–"

"And then what? How are you gonna find out for sure?"

"I dunno, Sue." She wasn't talking to me now, just at me. I could almost hear the wheels turning in her tiny little mind. She had to devise a plan, had to learn the truth somehow, had to catch Peter in his treachery. "I'll figure it out. I'm sorry to've bothered you about this."

"I'm sure it's nothing, honey. Just–" My phone beeped. Bonnie had hung up.

"The lipstick's probably Maria's," Peter explained. "She probably left it in the car on purpose. You know how she is. She's nuts."

Maria, like Stacy's long ago high school beau, lived out of town. She only visited Peter a couple times a year, and never believed him when he said he was single. If it was her lipstick – she was marking her territory.

"So you are cheating on Bonnie!" I said in amazement.

"I'm not, actually. Not with anybody but you." Peter pulled me over onto the bed, killing aliens or whatever it was he'd been accomplishing on his game system now forgotten. "I just saw Maria for lunch the other day. I haven't seen her in three months, and she was bitchy, showing all that crazy jealousy, like we're married or something. *How many girls are you stringing along now?"*

"Latinas are always jealous." I wondered what that emotion might be like. A jealous thought has never crossed my mind. My body, as the saying could be paraphrased, is jealousy-bone free.

"Whatever. She lives with some guy in San Diego, but she acts like she owns me, whenever she decides to breeze into town." Peter grinned, kissed me. "Like just because I've occasionally been her sancho, I'm supposed to be waiting for her. That possessive shit is an immediate turn off. Maybe it works for Mexican guys, but Maria's too crazy for this white boy. And now it seems like Bonnie's losing her mind, too." Peter shook his head at the ridiculousness of it all. "Christ, Sue! There are women in the world. I talk to them, have lunch with them sometimes. What's wrong with that?"

"Maybe you should explain to Bonnie–"

"Maybe she shouldn't be a jealous lunatic." Peter kissed me again, smiled. "Why are they all nuts, in one way or another, except for you?"

"I guess that's just your cross to bear."

I kissed him back, ran my fingers through his straight, red hair. I should've asked him if he was gonna call our little stepsister; I should've asked him what he was gonna do to

33

soothe her panic. But I didn't. I didn't want to talk about Peter's women and their suspicions anymore. I just wanted to do what came naturally, and he did, too.

BONNIE'S JOURNAL, PART TWO

Ah, yes. Peter. How I loved Peter! Until that day I found the lipstick in his car.

Susan tried to help, tried to reassure me, tried to explain it all away. She said he was probably telling the truth, that he was just tired, and that's why I hadn't seen him in three days, except for lunch. He'd probably just given some girl from work a ride home; that's where the cheap cosmetic had come from.

It was all harmless, innocent. Why didn't I just ask him about it?

All that was easy for Susan to say. Peter was her brother – what difference did it make to her who he gave rides to? But he was my boyfriend, and I loved him completely. I thought maybe we might get married someday. I used to daydream about it in class – happily ever after, just me and him, and maybe a couple of precious redheaded babies. Someday.

So it mattered to me if he was giving rides to strange women. Rides could lead to other things. It just wasn't seemly. If it was all as innocent as Susan theorized, why hadn't he mentioned it to me? The nausea in my stomach told me differently. It wasn't innocent at all. Peter was cheating on me. The surety of it made me want to die.

Susan advised me to call him, so a half an hour or so after I'd talked to her, I did. It was late, like eleven o'clock, and I really shouldn't've disturbed him, since he claimed to be tired from work, but I couldn't sleep. I had to see him.

When he answered the phone, he was lazy and slow-talking from sleep. But he didn't seem to be bothered that I'd awakened him. I told him that I was just lying there thinking of him, about how much I missed him. He said that he was sorry that he'd been preoccupied with work, and like a thoughtful boyfriend, he said he'd just hop in the shower, and then he'd be right over.

I guess I gave myself away by being too curious about the job thing. I asked too many questions, demanded too many explanations. He said the project he'd been assigned was some kind of large housing development, several hundred units, and it was gonna be a big payday for his company once all the permits were approved, and since when was I ever interested in what he did for a living?

"I just wanted to know what's been keeping you from me, that's all."

Peter sighed. I always hated it when he sighed, because it was his all-inclusive depiction of annoyance. Whatever he would say next – it wouldn't be his words, as much as his tone – I'd know for sure that he was pissed at me.

"I can't be here every night, Bonnie. I have to–"

"Why not?" I said, too quickly. "I love you, Peter. I miss you when you're not here."

"I have to decompress sometimes." Then, almost as an afterthought, he added, "I love you, too." But the annoyance remained.

"You could come and live here."

"I'm not ready for that, Bonnie," he said flatly. "We've only been seeing each other for six months–"

"How long do you think you need? I'm ready now."

"I dunno."

His voice was so calm, and I was bizarrely reminded of that scene in *Silence of the Lambs,* when the doctor is explaining how Hannibal did some terrible murder. *"His pulse never got above 85."* That was Peter.

He didn't care how much I missed him, how much I loved him. He needed his space. He was emotionless. He was usually so warm and loving, but now that I examined it, Peter had still always been a little distant. Now that a decision about the future of our relationship was up for discussion – how had I not paid attention to this aspect of his personality before?

Emotionlessness – wasn't that the hallmark of a liar? I was sure he was cheating on me now. He didn't want to move in together because that would cut into his time with *her,* whoever she was, the owner of that hideous shade of crimson lipstick. Only tramps wore something that red. No wonder he was tired.

But I wasn't angry. I was distraught. Peter was everything to me. I had to know for sure. If it was innocent, like Susan had said, then I'd never suspect him again. If it wasn't . . . I didn't know what I would do. But I had to find out.

I asked him to stay, and he did. He didn't notice my tears after we made love. I just couldn't stop thinking of him being intimate with someone else. I was sad, I was disgusted. I couldn't get it out of my head, the picture of him smiling at some other girl, touching her, kissing her, behind my back. It was like a bad gif. It just played over and over, and I couldn't just swipe it away. My stomach roiled. I was heartsick. I had to know for sure.

You Can't Make an Omelet Without Breaking Some Eggs, or,
N-now Th-That That Don't Kill Me Can Only Make Me Stronger . . . Maybe

Neither Peter nor I ever realized how devious Bonnie could be. Neither of us would've ever guessed the lengths to which she would go, the depths to which she would stoop, in her quest to discover whether or not he was cheating on her. He wasn't, not really, not like she suspected, and in the final analysis – asylum humor, hee, hee – I think she would've been better off if she would've just let it ride. But *she had to know.* So she found out.

Our very own Sherlock Holmes waited until Peter was out of town for some meeting. He was at his company's home office near the beach for the day – he wouldn't just happen to stop home for lunch, and what with the traffic, he wouldn't even be back in town until after six that evening. I was at work, as were Mom and John. We might've stopped home for lunch, but then Bonnie wasn't investigating us, was she?

She skipped class, and while we were all out earning a living, Bonnie let herself into the house. She went up to Peter's room. She knocked over books; she pawed through sock drawers; she opened bedside tables. She snooped, she nosied, she spied. And she found exactly the proof of infidelity that she was looking for, even though Peter wasn't cheating on her with anyone he hadn't known for years before he'd even suspected that there might exist such a being as Bonnie Putman.

I got the call the minute I walked in the door after work. I think she timed it that way. Bonnie, always considerate, hadn't wanted to bother me with the horrible, awful truth whilst I was still sitting at my desk. The anticipation, the need to let it all out, must've nearly killed her. I guess she couldn't tell her friend Mona; she had to tell me. I was family to Bonnie, and this was a family thing, after a fashion.

I'll never forget the sobs. My stepsister was nearly incoherent. "It's all true, Susan! I went up to his room! He's got condoms and sex toys! I found a black negligee, wrapped up in tissue paper and a ribbon! He's seeing someone else behind my back!"

"Maybe it's for you," I told her quickly. It wasn't – my birthday was coming up, and her thoughtful, attentive boyfriend invariably bought me a book and/or some lacy underthing to mark the occasion.

"I don't wear slutty stuff like that!" Bonnie cried in outrage, and I just had time to think that perhaps that was one of the reasons why her beloved and her stepsister were still spending late nights together. But then she sobbed in naked agony, and it touched a chord of pity in me.

I felt her pain, even if I couldn't empathize with its cause – she believed she'd caught Peter, but she really had nothing. There were no signs of an actual other woman in his room – she didn't find any tubes of lipstick there, because, like I say, I don't wear a lot of make-up. Shouldn't all this vaunted love that Bonnie felt for Peter make her want to hear his explanation?

"I can't believe he's doing this to me, Sue!"

"Oh, honey, don't cry!"

Her tears stung me. It wasn't guilt – I didn't feel as if I was the cause of Bonnie's pain, or even that Peter was the cause of it. Bonnie knew nothing about anything that went on between us. She thought she'd caught him at something that in actuality didn't have one thing whatsoever to do with her. My pity for her – it was like the time she'd cut herself while chopping vegetables, had held up her bleeding fingers for me to see. I felt as if the wound was on me. Poor Bonnie!

39

"I didn't want to believe it, but . . . I just knew, Susan! Ever since I found that lipstick! I just couldn't get it out of my mind. And now . . . Oh, God, it hurts so bad!" Bonnie wept and I felt for her.

"It's gonna be okay, honey! I'm sure it's not what you think." Because it wasn't.

She tittered hysterically. "It's exactly what I think! He's got another girl! Oh, God! I love you, Susan! You be sure to tell him that I loved him, too!"

And then she hung up.

I'd had the chicken pox when I was about ten, and was more or less confined to the house for a week. I almost got hooked on one of those daytime soap operas then. What played out next was just like *As The World Turns Around The Restless,* or whatever it was called. All the manufactured drama, the danger, the pathos. All that was missing was the organ music.

I tried to call Bonnie back, but she wouldn't pick up. I tried to call Peter, but he was probably still en route from Orange County. I flew to Bonnie's apartment, the homey love-nest she'd set up just so she could be with my stepbrother. All that was for nothing now, all just ashes. I pounded on the door; of course, she didn't answer. Like it was all part of some tired, it's-been-done script, I had to scare up the manager, had to explain that I thought my sister might be trying to harm herself, before the woman would let me in.

The scene inside was also like cinema: the overturned bottle of pills, empty save for one or two. Bonnie, sprawled unconscious on the bed, a tear-soaked wad of Kleenex balled up in her limp hand. The note, thanking me and my mom for being family to her, telling John she was sorry, blaming Peter. A touch of originality – Bonnie had thrown in a little poetry, from *The Winter's Tale,* something she'd been covering in school. *I never wish'd to see you sorry; now I trust I shall.*

The apartment manager called 911. The paramedics stabilized Bonnie and transported her to the hospital. There was the tearful scene when she woke up, Mom and John asking over and over, *Why?* John turned white with anger when Bonnie told him why, and then there was the shouting in the hallway when Peter finally got back into town. John wouldn't permit him in to see Bonnie, even though I thought that was what she wanted most of all.

John called Peter a worthless son of a bitch, told him to pack his shit and get the hell out of his house. I was amazed that Peter didn't say that it wasn't John's house at all, but my mom's. Glenn had left it to her, and it was always more or less understood that she would leave it to him. He'd grown up in that house. All his memories, of his long-dead mother, of his also passed father . . . John had no right to throw Peter out of what was really *his* house.

They kept Bonnie under observation for a couple of days – transferred her to the psych ward, not unlike this place where I am – and by the time she had convinced them that she'd made a mistake, that she no longer intended to harm herself, Peter was gone.

I'd helped him pack, whilst my mom and John hovered at the hospital. He said he knew a guy at the beach that would put him up, a co-worker, actually, from the home office. He said that the commute back to Riverside every day would be a bitch, but maybe he could transfer down there.

He told me happy early birthday, and gave me the damning teddy he'd picked out. He kissed me goodbye. His car packed with the sum total of his life – he'd left all his furniture behind – Peter, just like the old saying goes, got the hell outta Dodge.

BONNIE'S JOURNAL, PART THREE

So, yeah. I was right. Peter was cheating on me.

When I found the evidence in his room – the sex toys and the condoms and that filthy nightie, all wrapped up as a gift for that slut who wore the red lipstick – I kind of overreacted to the pain. Nowadays, it's become like a story that I once heard about a terrible thing that someone did to someone else. Memories of past agonies have become just that. Memories. But at the moment when I discovered that it was all true, the pain was absolute. I couldn't stand it, not for another second.

I'd had some major stress over a Chemistry class the semester before. I just wasn't getting it, and Susan couldn't help me, and all the worrying about it, the trying to understand it, had given me insomnia. So I'd gotten myself a prescription for sleeping pills. I wound up dropping Chemistry – I know now that my major's definitely not gonna be any kind of science – so I didn't have trouble sleeping anymore.

But I still had the pills. So I opened one of the beers that that heartless, cheating bastard had left in my fridge, and I washed the whole bottle down with it. Sobbing, I wrote my note and laid down on my bed to die.

But my loving sister saved me. I'd been talking to her on the phone when I'd come to my decision, and having made up my mind what I had to do, I hung up on her. There wasn't any need for more words. But Susan didn't just think, "Oh, I'm sure she'll get over it." Instead, she came running to my apartment and made the landlady let her in. She found me, dying, and called the life squad.

Susan and Vanessa and Dad were there when I opened my eyes in the hospital. I had almost made the ultimate mistake, but Sue saved me from myself.

Peter tried to get in to see me that night, but Dad threw him out of the hospital. Sue brought me my phone the next day. She said, "How can you feel better if you can't check your Facebook?" and that's when Peter called. Sue had told him about how I'd found all the evidence in his room, and he said he'd had those things for years, before he'd even met me, and where did I think his always-ready supply of condoms came from? He said I could ask my sister – he'd never had any girls up to his room. Ever. And the negligee – that was supposed to be for me. He said he knew it wasn't really my thing, but he'd wanted to try something new.

I didn't believe a word of it.

After he was done defending himself, Peter said that he was sorry that I'd reacted the way I did. I was sorry, too. Finding out that he was being unfaithful to me, and with some whorish-lipsticked, nightie-wearing bitch, had hurt so much, but in the bright light of day, in the hospital, I'd realized that killing myself would've been dumb. Dad said, "Christ, baby, he's just a skinny redhead! You can do so much better, and the next guy – the best revenge is living good, Bonnie. Your next boyfriend'll be so much better than this asshole."

And he was right. But I'm getting ahead of myself.

Peter said he wished I'd said something to him before I just went on ahead and freaked out. He would've explained, just like he was explaining now. He said he was sorry, that he would always love me. But seeing as how I didn't trust him – he said it just like that – "Seeing as how you don't trust me, I think it would be best if we didn't try to go on with this. Don't you? I don't see how it would ever work now."

I'd attempted suicide over his betrayal, and he didn't see how it could ever work after that. I'd wanted to die because of his actions, and he was breaking up with me. Not begging for my forgiveness, not promising to make it up to me. If I'd held out any hope that it was all just a crazy misunderstanding (like

43

Susan had said), if I'd wanted to try to resurrect the love I'd once felt for him – he'd just shot it down, pew, pew, pew, like in one of his video games. He couldn't see how it would ever work now.

I was shocked, appalled. I thought that here was the real Peter, cold, distant, realistic. How could I have overlooked that this was how he actually was? How could I ever have loved him? The pain tried to reassert itself, the thoughts of the lonely road ahead without him tried to rush back into my mind. But he was right. I could never trust him again. He was a lying, two-timing, emotionless bastard. I concentrated on that fact and said, "I guess this is goodbye, then." Over the phone. While I was still in the hospital, while I still had an IV in my arm, after trying to kill myself over him.

"I'm sorry, Bonnie. I'm sure we'll talk soon."

But we never did.

Peter fled like a rat leaving a sinking ship. I've never spoken to him since, have never seen him. If the way he took off wasn't proof that it was all true, I don't know what proof is. For all I know, he went and moved in with her.

I gave up my apartment – it was too full of his memory – and as part of that *the best revenge is living good* thing, I moved back home with Dad and Vanessa and Sue, right into Peter's spacious old room. It didn't hold any memories for me – I'd only been in there the one time, when I'd uncovered the truth. Dad gave his furniture to Goodwill, and after a fresh coat of paint, and all my cute furniture – it was my room then.

In the days and weeks that followed, Susan was my rock. Anytime I'd start to get sad and sniffly, she'd tell me to study to take my mind off of him, or she'd suggest that we go out to the bar and have ourselves a drink. I knew everyone at *Mickey's,* and even though I'd stopped working there once I moved back home, it was still a fun place to hang out.

Susan had called it quits with that George guy. She was between boyfriends – that's what she called it – "We're just two modern girls, currently between boyfriends, looking for adventure." She was always upbeat like that, although sometimes I'd catch her staring blankly off into space, her beer and the band and all the fun we were having forgotten. When I'd nudge her, she'd smile at me again. I was glad she was there. Going out with Susan helped me to forget all about Peter and the horrible thing he'd done to me. It helped me to forget about my stupid, almost-permanent reaction to it.

And if it hadn't been for Susan insisting that we go out to the bar on the weekends, just to see what was cookin', just to see what might be available, then I never would've met Jay.

Many Times I've Been Alone, **and,**
Men are Like Buses, There'll be Another One Along in a Minute

I missed Peter.

I realized it with a kind of dumb surprise. He'd only been gone a month, and it wasn't like we didn't text and talk. But I woke up in the middle of a Friday night, and I stared at my closet, cut diagonally by the moonlight. I stared at the light and the shadow for a good long minute, waiting for the door to open, waiting for Peter to glide through it and climb into bed with me. Then I heard the laugh track, muffled, dim, through our old secret passageway. Bonnie was awake, watching some sitcom on TV.

Peter wouldn't be coming through the closet, not ever again, because my stepbrother, thanks to Bonnie, like Alice in the old movie – Peter didn't live there anymore. But sometimes, it seemed as though he could read my mind, even over the miles to Orange County. My phone beeped. *Y don't u come down 4 a visit? Andy's out of town.*

So I went, just like that, got up and got dressed and padded silently out of the house at ten o'clock at night. If anyone was looking for me in the morning, I'd just say I went for a drive. The next time I'd have a better excuse.

But there weren't too many next times. Peter requested and was granted that transfer, and a promotion, too. His new responsibilities consumed him; he was tired. And of course, most Friday nights, Bonnie dragged me out to that tiresome bar where she used to work.

We mingled, we met, we drank. We listened to the band. I suppose it was fun enough, although at the oddest times, I found myself missing Peter. It was definitely time for me to find a date.

Bonnie had come to that conclusion, for herself, almost immediately. Her all-consuming love for my stepbrother and her dire upset over his imagined infidelity were forgotten within a hilariously short time. How dead she would *still* be, I thought with amazement, had her ridiculous attempt succeeded. The old saw: a permanent solution to a temporary problem, and she would've been missing all this partying and living the high life.

I had a few nibbles, but no bites. None of the guys that approached us were even remotely my type. Chubsters, or itty bitty guys, full of themselves. I liked my men tall and lean, watchful and quiet, and it seemed like all of that kind had joined a swim team somewhere and left town.

Bonnie struck out, too. But she kept on plugging away, returning to that beery bar like the swallows to Capistrano, like the lemmings to the cliffs. Smiling and laughing, dimples all on display, she'd talk the hopefuls up, drink the cocktails they bought for her. But she never went home with any of them. There wasn't a redhead in the bunch.

I resurrected Stacy from the vault of memory one weekend, made up some story about my old high school friend visiting from another state. It was all fiction: Stacy might've still lived right around the block from us, for all I knew. But it was an excuse to ditch Bonnie for the weekend so I could go spend it with my stepbrother.

The classic sign of being on the rebound is a burning desire to get right back up on that horse, and Bonnie was walking around those days in her jodhpurs and her riding helmet, carrying a saddle and a crop. She was bound and determined to find herself a new man, ASAP. But she hadn't been having any luck at *Mickey's,* so I thought it would be safe to leave her on her own for one weekend. And of course, that had to be the one weekend when Bonnie met *him.*

She thought she'd hit the jackpot while I was gone. Doesn't it always happen like that? The moment your back is turned, the moment you take a minute for yourself, disaster strikes. If I'd heard his line when he picked her up, I probably would've seen through him, right then. But I had my own life to live, even if one part of it was a secret, and I was not on hand when Bonnie met Mr. Right. I couldn't be there every second to look out for her.

I did believe that she bore watching, however. The whole suicide attempt – and over something as insignificant as a tube of lipstick rolling around in Peter's car, a couple of sex toys and an imagined infidelity for which she had absolutely no proof – this had made it undeniably clear to me that cute little Bonnie was not quite all there. She'd seemed a trifle ditzy from the outset, way too caught up in romance and happily ever afters, but it got real when the paramedics clicked that gurney up and wheeled her out to the ambulance. That was where the rubber met the road for me. Bonnie had tried to end herself, and over nothing. She was unstable at best, and especially so about men. She needed looking after, a calmer head on the scene to mitigate her delusions about the wonderfulness of the opposite sex. Who knew how far around the bend she'd allow the next one to push her?

I arrived back at home on Sunday afternoon, smiling and sated. The thought occurred to me that someday I might even see the beach, but Peter and I had not left the apartment all weekend, so there was no tell-tale sunburn to make anyone suspected where I'd been.

Bonnie perfunctorily asked me if I'd had a good time visiting my old friend from high school. *You have no idea,* I thought, but didn't have time to dwell on what I'd actually been doing, or even make up a convincing story about it, because Bonnie didn't really care about my mythical reunion with Stacy. She wanted to talk about what *she'd* been doing. She had momentous news.

She handed me her phone and said, "Look what I found."

The photo was in black and white, and I was immediately put in mind of that picture Deidre had shown me of her boyfriend Donny, a million years ago. Not the nude one – this wasn't anything like that. I recalled that head shot, the one I'd thought for a stoned second was Peter. I also reflected that Paul Simon had been mistaken in the old song – *everything looks worse in black and white* – because the guy smiling out at me from Bonnie's phone was *stunning* in black and white.

I couldn't tell what color his eyes were, or his hair, although he was obviously not a blonde. His hair looked dark, but it might've been red, but sincerely, none of that mattered. He was startlingly young. I thought with amusement that Bonnie must've been cruising the local proms whilst I'd been out of town: this one never could've made it past the sign on the door to *Mickey's* that proclaimed, *You Must Be 21.*

"Christ, Bonnie! What is he, sixteen?"

She took her phone, smiled at the pic, handed it back to me, so I could look at it some more. "Oh, that's not him now. We were talking – I told him that I'd once been a cheerleader, so he sent me that pic of him from high school. He's eighteen in that one. Scroll through."

But I didn't immediately scroll through. Ah, eighteen! Hadn't Donny been about eighteen in those famous black and whites? What was it that they said about men reaching their sexual peak at that unfortunately young age? From that crusty and advanced pinnacle of years and experience – my early twenties – I didn't think it was true. But, hot damn, this guy showed all of the incredible virility of that time, when all desires are fresh, novel and exciting, when the world's just one great big bowl of cherries. *Ripe,* he looked, the epitome of masculinity: a strong chin, an absolutely delectable neck. His shirt was open, and a little chest hair peeped out. It had probably not been there the summer before.

He was an exceptionally good-looking *boy,* but it was the expression on his face that made him strikingly so. *Hey, baby, ya wanna?* he seemed to be saying. *I'm that fast horse that always wins this race.* It was a line from a song I'd heard once, and it fit him perfectly.

My God, he was cute! I was convinced that Bonnie had shown me this picture first for a reason: whatever he looked like now, it couldn't possibly be better than this. He might be older, more polished, in subsequent shots, but that confident, not-boyish-at-all sexuality on his pretty, boyish face – it was a moment out of time, passed, but surely not forgotten, not by him or anyone who'd ever met him.

Next was a selfie of him and Bonnie, in color. I saw that he was of an age with us; I guessed he might possible be as old as twenty-five, Peter's age. But that was the only thought I had of Peter. He completely slipped my mind, because green-eyed redheads were suddenly too familiar, too last season. What Bonnie had *found* was what was happening now: he had black hair and enormous blue eyes, dark, like a summer sky at twilight.

As was not unexpected, Bonnie's new friend was a shade thinner than is his black and white high school snap; perhaps he'd played sports then. But that incredible, come-hither-you-know-you-want-it smile remained, and it remained devastating.

He was obviously a player, and entirely too much man for simple-hearted, damaged Bonnie. Red flags went up immediately in my mind. She'd thought she'd been in love with pale, jade-eyed, serious, bookish Peter? This guy was every woman's dream of the blue-eyed, devil-may-care, consummately sexy boy-next-door. He surely elicited adoration from every girl he met. I even felt a tug of it myself, just from two pictures. Bonnie was in over her head already.

When I didn't speak, she took her phone back and gazed fondly at the screen. "His name's Jay. He's twenty-six."

Nearly five years older than my unstable stepsister. Undoubtedly, infinitely wiser.

"Isn't he something?"

He's something else, I thought. A horse of a different color, as the saying goes. Again, way too much man for

Bonnie. I wondered how many different shades of lipstick charming Jay had rolling around under the seat of his car.

BONNIE'S JOURNAL, PART FOUR

Susan was dumbstruck when I showed her Jay's pictures. Positively speechless at how cute he is. Maybe I should've known right then that there would be trouble ahead.

She'd gone to visit some friend from high school for the weekend, and I'd been bored without her, so I'd gone to *Mickey's* by myself. I was standing at the bar, chatting up the bartender, my friend Darrin. Then *he* just materialized there beside me. It was as if there was some kind of electricity in the air, suddenly, and I looked over and there he was.

"Hi," he said. "I'm Jay. What's your name?"

I wound up going back to a booth with him. We talked and laughed. He bought me drinks. About five girls came up and said hi to him, but after polite nods, he ignored them. They each got the message and didn't linger. Fascinating Jay was interested in *me,* and they knew it. I wondered how I'd gotten so lucky.

We closed *Mickey's* that very first night. I told Jay my whole life story – he glowered and said he'd kill Peter if he ever met him – and he told me his. He told me that he worked as a plumber, but his true ambition was to play music. He wasn't in a band, but he gave guitar lessons to augment his income. He said if I ever wanted to learn, he'd teach me for free.

I thought that I'd like to learn whatever Jay had a mind to teach me, anything at all, except the guitar. That was the only thing about him that didn't interest me. Unlike most girls, I'd never had a thing for musicians. The ones I'd met had mostly struck me as unkempt and sleazy. But not Jay. *He had it goin' on,* as my Dad always said. He was most impeccably put together.

He told me that he shared an apartment with another plumber, another musician, some guy he'd known all his life, and when Darrin announced last call, I waited for Jay to ask me if I wanted to go home to that apartment with him. I waited eagerly, impatiently. But he didn't ask me. It was really too soon. It wasn't what nice people did. It would've been unseemly.

We went out into the still night together. The silent town slumbered all around us, but I was wide awake. For the first time in months, since before I'd caught worthless Peter cheating on me, I felt alive.

Jay told me he'd had a great time, that he was *so* glad that he'd met me. He asked for my phone number, and gave me his. He called an Uber for me, and when the driver pulled up, he asked if I might like to meet him again the following night, so we could continue to get to know each other.

Of course I said yes, and he smiled at me. I would've gotten out of the cab right then and gone home with him if he'd changed his mind, just because of his smile. But he only kissed me quickly on the cheek and said he'd see me tomorrow. We waved at each other as the cab pulled away.

I tried to call Susan on Saturday to tell her about him, but my call went straight to voicemail. Her phone was probably off, the better to concentrate on catching up with her old friend. I'd get to tell her soon enough.

I spent most of the day trying on different outfits, even a few from Susan's closet. That was a weird bit of architecture there in Vanessa's house – there was really just one big closet, and it connected Susan's room to mine, like a secret passageway from a fairytale castle. I primped and perfumed, and met Jay at *Mickey's* at eight. Then we went out to a late dinner, and then we went over to *The House of Ale,* because Jay liked live music, and he said the bands were always better at *The House of Ale.* I didn't even notice the band. I just noticed him.

We stayed out all night again, but again, he didn't invite me back to his place. He gave me an awesome kiss goodnight, however, so I could tell he was still interested. It was glorious! I wanted to get to know him better. I wanted to know him *completely*. But he's a gentleman, and even though it already seemed like I'd known him forever, we'd really just met. It was too soon for such shenanigans.

The Load Out Revisited or,
Think of Me What You Will, I've Gotta Little Space to Fill

(To any possible future readers of this epic *getting better* epistle, I apologize for the ancient musical references, but they only play the oldies station in the day room. What I wouldn't give to hear a good modern tune!)

Bonnie brought Jay home to meet the parents within a week or so. Apparently, it was a spur of the moment thing, and I missed it, as I was visiting my co-worker, Carmen, at the hospital. She'd just had a baby, and I wondered fleetingly if I would ever find a man, make him my husband, and commence onto the road of family life like she had. I doubted seriously that I would; my relationships just didn't last. They all bored me sooner or later. It was a depressing thought, born out of loneliness. Even if it would end in heartburn – hee, hee – I needed to try again ASAP. I really needed to find a date.

When I got home, Mom told me that I'd just missed Bonnie and Jay, and wasn't he just adorable! I already knew that, from his pictures. John only said, "Salteesiak? What kind of a name is that?"

Bonnie asked me to meet her at *Mickey's* after work the following day. She called it *their place,* and I had to ask for clarification on that.

"The bar, silly! Where Jay and I met! How's Carmen and her baby?"

Bonnie didn't care about Carmen or her baby. She didn't even know Carmen. She was just being her normal, considerate, happy self. Happier now than I'd seen her since the heady, new-Peter days.

"Jay's so awesome, Susan! I'm just dying for you to meet him!"

She'd been dying one other time, I couldn't help but recall, over another guy she'd thought was awesome.

I beat Bonnie to the bar after work. Apparently, the traffic down University Avenue from school must've been a bitch, because she was usually prompt. I saw Mr. Awesome sitting at the bar, smiling and laughing with the bartender. I noticed that she was transfixed with him; a patron at a table waved to try to attract her attention, but she ignored him and his entire party.

Even from across the room, a kind of fairy glamour seemed to envelope my stepsister's new man. If he was stunning in throwback black and white, and attractive (if thinner) in current color, he was breathtaking in person.

I walked up and stood at the bar, a short distance away from him. He noticed me immediately, and stopped talking to the bartender in mid-sentence. She reluctantly glanced in my direction and asked me what I'd like to drink.

I was in a playful mood. I nodded at Bonnie's boyfriend and said, "I'll have whatever he's having."

He smiled and the invitation in it was heart-melting. He told the bartender, "Put it on my tab, then."

He gestured at a nearby table, and the bartender, miffed that he was now ignoring her, stalked off to make my drink. I followed him to the table; he pulled out the chair for me, like an old-timey gentleman.

We sat. He said, "Hi, I'm Jay. What's your name?"

Jay. I wondered what that stood for. Bonnie had known him for a week or so already; she said she knew his whole life story. His mom and dad were still happily married; he was a plumber by trade, a musician by avocation. He looked like a musician; he oozed a guitar player's knowing sensuality. But I couldn't imagine him with a pipe-wrench in his hand unless it was the ringing-the-doorbell scene from some formulaic porno.

He lived with some boyhood buddy, also a plumber, also a musician.

He'd told Bonnie all this, but somehow his real name remained a mystery. Was Jay short for James? Jason? Jamiroquai? Or something as pedestrian as Junior? What kind of a name was Salteesiak, anyway? The thought struck me that he was not what he seemed, not unlike Fitzgerald's mysterious, timeless Gatsby.

"I know who you are, Jay," I told him. "I've seen your picture. I'm Bonnie's stepsister. Susan."

I extended my hand, because I wanted to feel his. A plumber's hand would be rough, wouldn't it? He surely didn't look anything remotely like a plumber.

His handshake was firm and I don't know about plumberly, but his hand did have a guitarist's callouses. I knew because I'd had a whirlwind weekend with a guitarist once. Peter had laughed, called me a groupie.

But now, Peter, as well as that sexy musician, fled my mind. Neither of them could hold the oft-cited candle to Jay Salteesiak, looks-wise. He was stunning.

The quality of his *What's your name, pretty girl?* smile didn't alter one iota once I told him that I was his girlfriend's sister, and that disconcerted me. But I can't say as it surprised me. He'd bought me a drink, featured me with that killer smile; all the first steps to picking me up. It was what men that looked as good as he did *did,* and effortlessly. Bonnie who?

That ancient tune played in my head again, the same one that I'd thought of when she'd shown me his not-worse-in-black-and-white pic: *And though my lack of education hasn't hurt me none, I can read the writing on the wall.*

I saw another apartment, maybe his this time; another bottle of pills or maybe a razor blade and a blood-filled bathtub. Jay Salteesiak was no Prince Charming. He was a down to be dirty player, just like that multi-talented musician I'd entertained for a weekend, just like my *awesome* stepbrother, whom I'd entertained regularly since I was fifteen. I knew that Bonnie was dreaming of a happy home with a fireplace and a white picket fence, a couple of kids and happily ever after, and I was sitting across the table from the personification of *you can't turn a whore into a housewife.*

It was disturbing, and as they say in lolspeak, I had a fear then. A fear for my naïve little stepsister's fragile mental health. I could tell by just looking at his gorgeousness that Jay was the wrong man for Bonnie. The absolute *wrongest.*

She skipped into the bar then, all bright smiles and dimples. She kissed this bad, bad boy on his forehead, plopped down into his lap. I thought that this gesture was mighty familiar for the state of their affair – I knew she hadn't slept with him, or I would've heard about it, and all I'd heard was that he was a gentleman, that he hadn't even suggested it yet. He was a lot of things, irresistible not being the least of them, but I doubted seriously that he was anywhere in the neighborhood of being a gentleman. He was just playing at chivalry, just playing her.

"Do you think Susan looks like her picture?" quoth Bonnie.

Again, that killer smile. "Exactly," he said, his eyes never leaving mine. "I recognized her right away."

I strove to hide my astonishment. What was this, some kind of test? He'd *recognized me right away* as Bonnie's sister – had he tried to pick me up just to see if I'd go for it? If I was loyal to her? If I might want to test *him?* WTF?

Oh, yeah. Oh, no. This just wasn't going to do at all.

BONNIE'S JOURNAL, PART FIVE

Maybe I never saw any trouble on the horizon with Jay and Susan because, after her initial speechlessness at his pictures, she didn't have much to say about him. Not at first.

Mona, on the other hand, thought he was great. Her mom and dad had a granny flats at the back of their lot, and she and her boyfriend Tim had decided to move into it together. It had been uninhabited for a long time, and they scrubbed and cleaned and painted, just like newlyweds. But the first night, the old plumbing backed up. Not very romantic.

Mona called me to ask if Jay might have any advice on what to do to fix it. My wonderful boyfriend did it one better: he and I went over there to scope out the extent of the problem, and he just went ahead and fixed it for them, free of charge. Mona was so grateful, she gave him a big hug and a kiss. I didn't think Tim particularly liked that, but he was grateful, too. He slapped Jay on the back, genuinely told him thanks. We've had dinner at their place lots of times. We all get along great together.

Susan, on the other hand, always had some excuse whenever I invited her to dinner with Jay and me. She declined, every time I asked her. I figured she begged off because she felt like a third wheel, what with being single and all. Or maybe she just didn't like him. As it would turn out, she probably hated him from the very beginning. Or maybe not. Maybe it wasn't that at all.

But I really didn't dwell on Susan's dislike of Jay, real or imagined, because Mona and Tim's delightful domestic scene had gotten me thinking. I'd been to Jay's apartment by that time, when his roommate wasn't there, but still we hadn't been intimate. He hadn't even broached the idea of me spending the night with him, I think, because he was uncomfortable undertaking such activities, especially for the first time, with his roommate sleeping in the next room. Like I say, Jay's a gentleman. He told me that his roommate was single, just like Susan, and I thought that Jay didn't want to rub his buddy's nose in the fact that he wasn't anymore.

So all these life facts gave me an idea. Mom didn't know about my foolhardy suicide attempt. All she knew was that I'd broken up with Peter. She didn't even know that I'd given up my first place. I'd just told her that I'd found a fairly good job, and didn't need her to supplement my rent anymore. The truth was, except for the little bit of money Dad gave me every week, I was broker than the Ten Commandments, as Susan liked to say. I'd even blown through the proceeds from my returned security deposit, livin' la vida loca at *Mickey's.*

Still, I had a plan. I couldn't ask Mom for a big chunk of change again for another first and last, but I could tell her my rent had gone up, so she'd start depositing those funds again. It was just a small lie, and not only could she afford it, I knew it made her feel good to contribute to my life. That's why she's still paying my as yet major-less way through college.

So at dinner one night, I calmly broached the subject with Dad. I said I was feeling so much better these days, and was thinking about trying it on my own again. I told him that I could get my old job back at *Mickey's* – Dad loved the place, said it always reminded him of a bit more grown up *Applebee's.* I told him that if he could just lend me the money for the first and last and security deposit, I thought I was ready to take another stab at adulthood.

Dad glanced at Vanessa and Susan – there were surprised looks on both mother's and daughter's faces. Then Dad told me to let him sleep on it. I couldn't ask for more than that. The whole attempting to off myself thing had thrown him for the oft-mentioned loop, so I let the subject drop.

Later that night, Susan knocked on my door. I'd once suggested that she could always come in to see me through the cool closet that connected our rooms, but she never did. I told her to come in, and she was solemn and serious and started in on me immediately.

"You want to move out so you can be with Jay, don't you?"

The ghost of what Peter had done to me hung in her eyes. I thought it was sweet that she was concerned about me. But Jay was nothing at all like Peter, and besides . . . I giggled.

"I haven't even been with Jay yet."

"What a great way to break in a new apartment," she said crudely.

"I don't know why you stay here," I countered, off topic.

"Because it's rent-free," she returned harshly. "Where would I go?"

"Anywhere you wanted to go." It was sweet that she wanted to look out for me, but I didn't like her tone. "Why don't you let Dad and Vanessa spend their golden years alone together? Maybe they'd like that."

"We're not talking about them, and we're not talking about me. We're talking about you. Why don't you just let it ride for a while? Make sure you're not just liking this dude because you're on the rebound? Make sure you're really–"

"It's been six months, Susan. I'm over Peter." It didn't even hurt to say his name anymore.

I could tell that she didn't believe me, but seriously, when did she become my keeper?

"Two things," I said. "First, it's all up to Dad. I can't do it unless he lends me the money. And secondly, Jay has his own place. It's not like we'd be moving in together."

Although that would've been the greatest thing ever. Another giggle escaped me. I hadn't even slept with Jay yet, but I would've been willing to move in with him. He was exactly perfect, and wasn't that how things were done, once upon a time? Didn't people used to get married and set up a life together before they'd even considered going to bed?

Susan looked even more worried, so I told her, "I'm a big girl, Sis. Everything's gonna work out great."

He's So Fine, There's No Telling Where The Money Went, or, If It Looks Like a Duck, Swims Like a Duck, and Quacks Like a Duck, Then It's Probably a %^&*# Duck

If John had been my first stepfather, I could've gone to him. If John had been Glenn, I could've told him not to give Bonnie the money. I could've confided my fears, if Glenn had been her daddy, told him that I didn't think she was ready to try it on her own again. I could've told him exactly what I thought about her good-looking boyfriend, how I thought he was just the wrong type for her.

But John wasn't Glenn. He'd never been overly friendly with me, and after the brouhaha over Peter, he was even colder. I didn't think for a second that he suspected anything between my stepbrother and myself, but Peter *was* my stepbrother. We'd grown up together for many years, whereas Bonnie and her lovesickness were newcomers into my life. I think, in John's eyes, there was some kind of guilt by association – since I was part of the package that had included Peter, maybe I wasn't to be trusted either.

So I didn't say anything to John, or to Mom. Maybe Bonnie was right, maybe they wanted to spend their golden years alone, so maybe Mom was glad to be one step closer to that, as she would be if Bonnie moved out again. Maybe Mom was thinking she wouldn't overly miss me if I took off, too.

But maybe all that was just a product of my loneliness, of my feeling sorry for myself. Mom didn't want me gone. She loved me.

LM Foster

John gave Bonnie the money. Everything that happened wouldn't have happened otherwise. I wouldn't now find myself in a locked-down mental health facility, scribbling my life story in a wide-ruled, child's notebook, to help myself to *get better.* To keep myself from sincerely losing my mind.

But it is what it is.

Since Bonnie had been seeing Mr. Right, I'd been at loose ends on the weekends. Peter had moved in with that chick, was playing all monogamous, so I couldn't even go visit him. We still texted though, and he said he missed me. That was a bright spot.

I must've looked sad, because Carmen from work invited me over for dinner, the Friday after Bonnie's announcement that she wanted to be free again. I went, because I liked Carmen. She had a nice husband and an adorable baby and a settled family life, so different from the teapot tempests at my house. My stepfather didn't like me. My stepsister was about to make another huge mistake. I missed my stepbrother. It was nice to be around normal people.

So I didn't hear about what had occurred until the following morning.

I came outside to greet the day, and found Bonnie sitting in the backyard, drawn and angry-looking, staring out past the back gate at the alley that ran behind our house.

Without so much as a *Good morning,* she said, "We got robbed last night."

I imagined some kind of heist at *Mickey's,* guns and masked men, *Everybody put your hands in the air, this is a stick-up!* I even asked, "Was anybody hurt? How much did they get?" before I remembered that Bonnie hadn't gone back to work at *Mickey's* yet.

She gave me a withering look, as if I was simple, and was annoying her with my stupidity. "Not at the bar. Right here."

Bonnie told the tale. Just before Mom and John went out to dinner – Mom kept her marriages alive, I reckoned, by insisting on regular date nights – John had presented his daughter with an envelope stuffed with money. Fifteen hundred

64

dollars cash American. Six for the first and six for the last, and three for the security deposit on her new digs. John had wished her luck in her new endeavor, then had taken his bride out for eats.

Bonnie had immediately called Jay with the good news. He came over; Bonnie was waiting for him in the backyard.

She recited the details of what happened next in a slow, exacting tone, and like a court reporter, I record them here, verbatim.

"It was just getting dark. Jay came through the gate, gave me a big squeeze, told me how excited he was for me. The money was sitting right here on the table, in the envelope. I asked him if he wanted a soda. He said sure, so I went inside to get it for him.

"I opened the fridge and took out a Coke. I looked up and he was standing right there. He hugged me again, kissed me . . . He whispered that he was glad I was gonna have a place soon, so we could at last be alone."

A ghost of a smile curved Bonnie's lips. "I said, 'We're alone right now.' And that was all it took, Susan. We went up to my room . . ."

How karmic that must've been for her, I thought, how positively *what goes around comes around*. Nailing the blue-eyed wonder boy in Peter's old room. How ya like dem apples, Pete? Right there in the very place she and her histrionics had gotten him kicked out of.

But maybe it wasn't so wonderful after all. Bonnie wasn't smiling.

"We couldn't have been gone for more than a half hour, Sue. When we came back downstairs – the back door was still open. We came back out to sit here again. The money was gone."

I was dumbstruck; for a minute I couldn't fathom what she had said. It just didn't click.

"Someone must've seen it on the table, and as soon as we went in the house, they must've come in and taken it."

"Who would've–"

"Some bum. In the right place at the right time."

I tried to piece together what she was telling me. We'd had the random bum, the occasional shopping cart pusher, wander down the alley before. And three bags of aluminum cans left just inside the back gate overnight had disappeared once, when I was a teenager. I'd been pissed about that incident. I'd saved up those cans, was planning on buying a CD or something with the money I was going to get for being a good citizen and recycling them.

But that had been years ago, and the booty had been right there by the alley. All the thief had had to do was reach over the low fence. And it was just cans – maybe they thought the big green bags had been put there out of a sense of charity, that they'd been left just for an unfortunate in need of a quick buck or two.

But we were talking about fifteen hundred bucks now. I do believe that amounts to grand theft. And the person or persons would've had to come all the way into the yard . . .

"Did you see anybody? Did you hear the gate squeak?"

Bonnie shook her head. Even though the gate was squeaky, and all the lights were on and the back door was open, and the thief had to be eagle-eyed enough to spy a white envelope on a white table all the way from the dark alley, had to be ballsy enough to dare the distance and the squeaky gate and the light and the possibility of immediate apprehension – of course, Bonnie and Jay had seen no one, had heard nothing. First they were busy making out in the kitchen, then they were busy getting busy in my stepbrother's old room.

"You were only gone a half hour?"

"Maybe it was only twenty minutes. Jay was nervous. He thought Vanessa and Dad might come home at any minute. It was great, but . . . it was quick." Bonnie gazed out at the alley again, devoid though it was of any nefarious types.

Damn, I thought, *what a way to start things out.* Only a quickie with the man of her dreams for the first time, and robbed of her new apartment money, too. Man, what a downer!

66

I thought I should offer some words of comfort, but for the span of a good half a minute, nothing came to me. I rejected, *If it weren't for bad luck, you'd have no luck at all,* because this wasn't the time for humor. It was just an awful break.

At last I said, "What did John say? Did he call the cops?"

Bonnie featured me with that bitterly annoyed look again. She gestured at the table as if it was the table's fault that her dumb ass had left an envelope full of cash laying out in the open while she all so briefly nailed Speedy Salteesiak. "What're the cops gonna do? Take fingerprints?"

I shrugged. She was right. The cops weren't going to do a damn thing.

"I already called Jon this morning."

Jon owned *Mickey's*. Or if he didn't own it, he was the manager. The boss.

"He said I could have my old job back. He even said he'd lend me the money up front, let me work it off. I'm picking it up later, so I'm still moving out tomorrow." Bonnie gave me a thin smile.

Apparently, her luck wasn't so bad, after all. *Whoever you are, I have always depended on the kindness of strangers.* Another classic that Bonnie was covering in school. With her dreams of a new love-nest, this time with Jay – and I knew Jay was far, far worse than Peter – I thought that Bonnie was living in the same kind of fantasy world as Blanche DuBois. And just like Blanche, I was sure that my stepsister was going to wind up in the Ha Ha Hotel.

Funny how it was me that wound up here. Oh, well. It's not forever. I'll convince the doctor that I'm *better,* the moment I get in to see him.

Bonnie and I sat in silence for a few more minutes. John came outside and resolutely proceeded down the walkway toward the alley, on his way to *Home Depot* to purchase a lock for the gate. The old chestnut about the cows having already escaped played through my mind. What was the next thief gonna steal? No one was going to leave envelopes full a cash laying around again.

Just to be sure, just to be funny, I suggested to Bonnie, "Maybe you should have Jon write out a check for your new landlord."

I expected another withering glance, but then Jay pulled up and parked in the cursed, thief-harboring alley, and of course, Bonnie brightened immediately. He came up the walk, looking appropriately sullen and angry about the theft, but he still had time to flash me one of his killer smiles.

It's all good, Sue, he seemed to say. *It's only money. Ya wanna take a ride with me, and not talk about it at all?*

Then he beamed the same invitation to my stepsister and she returned his smile. How *could she not see* that he gave the same come-hither look to me that he did to her? How could she not realize that if she suddenly had to run to the store, and she left me and her *boyfriend* alone, that a pass from him wouldn't be far behind? I could see. Bonnie and I and all the other women in the world were interchangeable to Jay, and I wondered how long it would take her to catch him making the trade.

They left for brunch, and since Mom was busy in the house somewhere, and John wasn't there to overhear me, I gave Peter a call.

"Maybe it's a good thing you moved to the beach," I told him. "The old neighborhood's gone to the dogs since you left. Crime rates have skyrocketed."

I told him about Bonnie's new man; he said, "Good for her." I told him that I thought Jay was the wrong type for Bonnie, and he had no comment about that. Then I told him about her plans for a new place and about the tragic theft.

Peter was silent for a long time, then said, "Let me get this straight. She went in first, left the money on the table. Then he followed her, and they were right there in the kitchen, lights on, door open?"

"Then they went up to your room." I giggled.

This gem bothered him not at all. "Yeah, but the thief didn't know that. They might've come back out at any second."

"Maybe he waited."

"He still could've gotten caught. That's a big risk."

"It was fifteen hundred bucks, Pete."

"I dunno. I don't think it was some bum who just happened to be walking down the alley."

"Who then?"

Another pause. "You're kidding, right?"

I asked him what he was trying to say, and he laughed, that old, throaty, desultory Peter chuckle. "Think about it for a second. Bonnie went in the house first, leaving him out there with the money. He just stuck it in his pocket, Sue."

Immediately, I said, "He would never–"

"How do you know? Didn't you say you think this guy's a player? How do you know he's not a thief, too? It had to've been him. Thieves don't just wander up into lighted backyards where the door's open, just to see what they might come across."

"Maybe someone was watching them . . ."

"How unlikely is that? He did it, Sue. It couldn't've been anybody *but* him. Little Bonnie's new swain is a stone cold thief."

Now I was silent. I didn't like Jay, not one bit. I was sure that he would hurt Bonnie, probably sooner rather than later. But I'd never pictured him as a thief.

"I've got to tell her."

"I would," Peter agreed. Then he said suddenly, "I miss you, baby," and I forgot about Bonnie and her bad choices. Peter's roommate-girlfriend must've been out of earshot, because he only called me *baby* when he was sure he wouldn't be overheard. "You've gotta come down and see me again sometime."

"We'll go to the beach."

"That's doubtful, don't you think?"

It was. He probably went to the beach with What's-her-name. Peter and I, we didn't have time for the beach.

"Say the word, my brutha," I told him. I called him *my brutha,* regardless of who overheard me. It reinforced the sibling illusion, did it not? "My calendar's clear these days," I added.

"Keep looking, Sue. I'll call you soon. Keep looking out for Bonnie, too. Warn her about this asshole."

What else did I have to do?

BONNIE'S JOURNAL, PART SIX

My dad is the greatest dad in the world.

He came through with the money for my new apartment, a big thick envelope full of crisp hundreds and fifties and twenties. I called Jay with the good news, and he came over to congratulate me.

But having the greatest dad in the world hasn't kept me from being the dumbest daughter in the world. I left the money sitting on the table in the backyard, and when my attention was diverted, someone snuck in and stole it.

It was Jay's fault that my attention was diverted. I'd gone inside to get him a soda, and he followed me into the kitchen. He told me he was glad I was getting my own place, so we could finally be alone, and then one thing led to another – Dad and Vanessa weren't home – so I took him by the hand and led him upstairs to my room.

I thought it was adorable that he was nervous for our first time together. Nervous was something that Peter had never been – he was always such a conceited, superior son of a bitch, so sure he was God's gift to women. Ha! Compared to Jay, he's nothing but a skinny redhead, just like my Dad said.

Anyway, while it was glorious and great, Jay was worried that my father might come home at any minute, so our first time was quick. Since then, well . . . words can't really describe him, but if I had to try to pick just one, it would be . . . magnificent!

After our cute quickie, we went back outside, and after talking for a few minutes, we discovered that my rent money was gone.

Jay waited with me until Dad and Vanessa got home. Dad was PISSED, but he wasn't mad at me for leaving the money out there on the table so much as he was mad at the sad state that the world's coming to these days. You can't even duck inside the house to get a Coke without being robbed.

The next morning, I called Jon, my old boss at *Mickey's*. I told him what was going on, that I needed my job back, because I was moving out on my own again. He said that he'd missed me, that he needed the help, so I could start right away. I told him about the robbery, and just like my dad's the greatest dad in the world, I found out right then that Jon's the greatest boss in the world. He said he'd lend me the money that had been stolen, and I could pay him back out of my check a little at a time. I felt like the luckiest girl alive!

I was sitting in the backyard when Sue came outside. She'd been out somewhere the night before, had come in after we'd all gone to bed, tired from the not-fun excitement. So she didn't know that we'd been robbed.

She was shocked, of course, but happy for me when I told her that Jon was going to lend me the money, and everything was still on for the new place. She had no comment when I told her that Jay and I had finally . . . been intimate.

Jay came to pick me up for brunch, and he was also amazed at Jon's generosity. When we went over to the bar to pick up the check, Jay shook Jon's hand and thumped him on the back and told him what a great guy he was. Jon looked at little embarrassed, but I could tell that Jay's gratitude made him feel good. Jay has that talent – he always knows the right thing to say to everybody.

To celebrate my new freedom, Jay and I took a ride up to the mountains. He dropped me back off at the house about sundown, and Susan appeared to be sitting in the exact spot where I'd left her that morning. She didn't smile when I got out of Jay's car, didn't return his wave.

She didn't ask me if I'd gotten the money from Jon. She just said, "I've been thinking about this theft, Bonnie. How it had to've gone down."

Obviously. She'd been sitting in the backyard all day. What else did she have to do?

"Follow me for a minute, will ya?"

I said okay. It was sweet that she had taken such an interest in my troubles.

"It was about this time?"

"Later. It was already dark."

"And you were sitting here, facing the alley, waiting for Jay. But you didn't see anyone walk by?"

I shook my head.

She went through the whole thing. I could tell that she'd rehearsed the scenario, probably dozens of times, the exact words she would use, the airtight logic. Jay sat here, the money was there. She used her cellphone to represent the missing cash.

"You went into the house first? How long before he followed you?"

"A couple seconds. Long enough for me to get a soda out of the fridge." Wasn't she cute? This was just like *CSI*.

"What was he wearing?"

"Who?"

"Jay!"

"Oh. I dunno. His hoodie, probably."

"The one with the pocket in front?"

"Yes, Susan. All hoodies have a pocket in front."

"And when he hugged you, you didn't feel anything bulky? In the pocket?"

My smile evaporated. "What are you trying to say, Sue?"

"He did it, Bonnie."

Maybe this was the first indication that she was losing her mind. Maybe I should've seen it right then.

She took in my shocked expression and went on quickly. "Go with me on this. It couldn't've been anyone but him. If someone came in from the alley when you were in the kitchen, you would've heard the gate." She opened it. It squeaked.

"They must've come in while we were upstairs."

Susan whirled and dramatically pointed at the second story. "Your window's open. You would've heard it. I went up there. I had Mom open and close the gate. You can hear it."

"Did you tell Vanessa that you think Jay stole–"

"No. I just told her I was trying to figure it out. But he did it, Bonnie. No one else came into the yard. You would've heard them."

"We were kinda preoccupied . . ."

Susan shook her head. She had an answer for that, too. "You said Jay was nervous, worried that John would come home and catch you. He would've been listening for the gate. He stole that money, Bonnie."

"Will you stop saying that!" I yelled. "Jay didn't steal anything. Maybe they jumped over the gate, or . . . Look." I pushed it open very slowly, stealthily, and while it still squeaked, the sound was barely audible.

Again she shook her head. "Phantom bums, spying on you from the alley, sneaking in here while you left the door open, when you were just inside? Why didn't they just come in and steal the TV? It doesn't add up, Bonnie!"

"You're crazy, Susan!" I said, and now, I wish I would've realized how right I was. "Why would Jay steal from me?"

"Why not? It's not like you know him."

"I know him enough to know he's not a thief."

"Do you? You don't." Susan shook her head a third time, like a stubborn child. "Have you ever heard of–" and then she said *Oscar's Radar* or something.

When I shook my head, she snatched her phone off the table, scrolled. *"A problem-solving principle, attributed to . . . Franciscan friar, scholastic philosopher and theologian . . ."*

Or something like that. She was just babbling now.

"Right here. *Among competing hypotheses, the one with the fewest assumptions should be selected."*

I didn't know what any of that meant, and Susan sighed. Her sigh showed all her annoyance with me, just like her brother's did.

"It means that in any situation, the simplest solution is usually the correct one. In this case, the solution that says that some mysterious, peeping Tom spied the money on the table from all the way out in the alley, in the dark, then snuck in here and stole it while you guys were right inside – that's not the simplest solution. Not by a long stretch. The simplest solution is that your new boyfriend is a thief." When I still didn't respond, she added, "Just think about it for a while, Bonnie. You'll see that I'm right. It couldn't've been anybody but him."

Susan went into the house, and I sat down at the table and thought about it. As God is my witness, I thought about it, looked at it from all angles, because Susan was my sister. She loved me, and she was just looking out for me. She'd always been so much calmer, so much more logical than me.

I thought about coming right out and asking Jay, "Did you take my money?"

But if he did, he surely wasn't going to cop to it. And if he didn't, then he'd be hurt that I'd even suspect him of such a thing. He'd be devastated that I'd even put it into words. It would ruin our relationship before it even got started.

I sat out in the backyard for a long time, mulling it all over. I finally came to the conclusion that there was no way that I could ever know for sure, one way or another. This situation wasn't like the one with Peter. I'd had him red-handed. Crimson lipsticked. But the cash was gone, and it wasn't like Jay was going to go flashing it around if he had taken it. It wasn't like I had access to his ATM records, or access to his mattress, if he'd hidden it under that.

It was a paradox, a conundrum. There were not enough variables to solve for x, or too many. However that works. Like science, I've never been any good at math.

Jay was wonderful, I knew that much for sure, so I decided to take the advice that Susan had given me on other issues, if not on this particular one. I decided to *let it ride.*

It Must've Been Some Other Body, No, No Child, It Wasn't Me

Bonnie tricked me.

She called, all aflutter, said she was at Jay's place, but her car wouldn't start, and he wasn't home, and she had to make it to study group or she was gonna flunk, and Jay wasn't picking up, could I please come over there and get her and give her a ride up to school?

It was the mantra of my life right then: what else did I have to do?

So she texted me his address, there at the foot of Mt. Rubidoux, and I hurried over to fetch her, like a good stepsister. She told me to come up – she was having trouble locating her notebook.

Bonnie opened the door and grinned sheepishly at me, bade me come in. I discovered that Jay's apartment was a nice, big place, and I wondered if he was a few months ahead on the rent, seeing as how I was sure that he was fifteen hundred dollars to the better right then.

And there was the man himself, sitting on the couch, tuning a black and white guitar. As always, he smiled at me.

"I'm sorry, Susan," Bonnie said. "I told a fib. I don't have study group tonight, and the car's fine. I just wanted you to come to dinner. I'm making Mexican. I knew you'd have some excuse not to come if I just invited you over here."

I had absolutely no response to that. She was correct, but I didn't want to admit it, and I was also amazed at how devious she'd become lately, thinking up ruses and lies. Maybe Jay's corruption was rubbing off on her. She'd conned her mother into paying for her new place, again, and she'd conned me into showing up at her thieving boyfriend's apartment for dinner. I was speechless.

Jay held up the guitar, asked my opinion of his *axe,* and I thought he was an amateur indeed, because no one used that word anymore. That's what my professional musician friend had told me, anyway.

"Is it new?" I asked, because all those missing dead presidents were asking the same thing in my head.

"What did I tell you?" Bonnie said with a breathless giggle.

"I've had this guitar since high school, Sue. Ah, if it could talk, the stories it could tell!"

He gave me a smoky wink, inviting me to speculate on the doors that his good looks and an ability to play guitar had no doubt been routinely opening for him since he'd learned to be a musician.

But I didn't have time to consider all that, because I was again struck stupidly silent by the idea that idiot Bonnie had *told* him that I suspected him of the theft. By doing so, she'd made us adversaries, and that was not the position in which I wanted to find myself. I didn't like Jay, but I didn't want him to know it. Now he'd be watchful and suspicious of me; he'd try to hide his true colors, because he knew I'd be reporting my observations back to my stepsister. Why did she have to be so damn dumb?

I glared at her, but she just shrugged, offered me a prim *Honesty is the best policy* look. A timer sounded in the kitchen, and she went to check on dinner.

Jay was looking down at his guitar when he said, "How could you think that about me, Sue? That I would steal from Bonnie? That's a helluva fucked up accusation. Why do you have it in for me? What've I ever done to you?"

He didn't raise his voice, didn't even meet my eyes. It was all matter of fact. He didn't really care about my suspicions, because it was obvious that Bonnie didn't think he'd taken the money, and her opinion was the only one that mattered. It was clear that she'd made it all into a big joke. *My sister thinks you're a thief. Isn't that crazy?*

"I was just trying to work out all the possibilities," I replied. That sounded lame, even to me. "I try to not base my opinions on what I think, only on what I can prove." *Unlike your hysterical girlfriend.* "And I can't prove you took it. So, I don't have it in for you, Jay. Don't think that."

What possible good could it do to have him know that I didn't trust him? Why, I thought again, did Bonnie have to be so stupid as to tell him that I didn't?

"That's good, Sue. Because I want us to be friends." He looked up then, skewered me with those incredible blue eyes. "I like you."

There was a heartbeat, then another, whilst he held my gaze and allowed me to consider all the possibilities of what being *liked* by Jay Salteesiak could entail. I found that I couldn't look away.

Then Bonnie flounced out of the kitchen, all aflutter for real this time. "The Tapatio must've fallen out of the bag in the car!"

She opened the door and rushed out to retrieve the invaluable Tapatio, and the door slammed behind her. It locked. She'd have to knock to get back in. She wouldn't be able to accidentally interrupt . . . What had that smug son of a bitch been saying about *liking me?*

I looked away from the door to discover that he'd set his guitar against the couch and was now standing up. I thought it strange that I'd never noticed how tall he was before. He took a step forward, put his hand on my shoulder.

"I like you so much, in fact, that I've got a surprise, just for you."

He seemed to lean in toward me, and I thought, *Go ahead and kiss me, you bastard. I'll kiss you back, just to see what it's like. But if you think I won't tell her, you've got another think coming. You think she won't catch us because the door's locked, but I'll tell her. 'Your slick boyfriend tried to kiss me,*

Bonnie, the very second your back was turned!' I won't be a party to your fucked up little game . . .

But Jay didn't kiss me, although I'm entirely convinced that he wanted me to think he was gonna do exactly that. He leaned in, then farther, past me, and retrieved his phone from the end table. He pushed a button, held it to his ear, all the time smiling languidly at me.

"Where are you, my pet?" he said into the phone, then looked over at the door when there came the sound of a key scrabbling in it. "Your timing, as always, is perfect," Jay added, then hung up.

The door opened and a blonde guy walked in, followed by Bonnie, clutching her precious bottle of Tapatio. She skittered back out to the kitchen – she had to've, because she came back out from that direction later. But Bonnie, and Jay, too, for that matter, had entirely ceased to exist to me.

I think I might've gasped, because the guy that walked in ahead of the industrious chef was *extraordinary.* He was taller that Jay, who was certainly tall enough. His impossibly straight, white-blonde hair was parted in the middle. It fell almost to his shoulders, like some throwback rock star. Jay's eyes put you in mind of summer's dusk, dark and almost purple-blue; this one's eyes were also blue, but like a spring morning, clear and light and bright with possibilities.

"Don't call me your pet, Jay, you asshole," quoth this vision, and immortal poetry rang in my head: *Teach not thy lips such scorn, for they were made for kissing . . .* God, his mouth! It was flawless. *He* was flawless.

Jay patted me lightly on the shoulder. "I'd like you to meet my best friend and partner in crime, Sue. This is Treavor." He introduced me as Bonnie's sister, and I didn't even think to correct him, because I was shaking Treavor's hand and it was rough and calloused like Jay's, like a guitar-playing plumber's would be, and *Christ,* he was fine!

"Nice to meet you, Sue."

For another split-second all I could think of was more verse, from the same play: *Now is the winter of our discontent made glorious summer by this sun of York.* Oh, Blondie, will you be my sun, perhaps as soon as tonight?

I got a grip and my Shakespearean fugue passed. (Bonnie always said it, and she was right, if I say so, myself – I would've made an exemplary English major, if I'd ever had the time for something as pointless as college.)

I said it was nice to meet Treavor, too. It was *damn* nice.

BONNIE'S JOURNAL, PART SEVEN

I guess if I was the type to feel sorry for myself, I might dwell on the bad things that happened in my life, all in a very short time. There was Peter's cruel betrayal, and my hasty reaction to it. And there was the theft of my rent money – I wound up with two debts behind that. And of course, there's this terrible thing with Susan and Jay.

But I don't dwell on these bad events, because the good things that occurred in between were great. I met Jay, and I got my new pad, despite being robbed. Jay and I are in love, and we're planning to get married someday. He's the best guy in the world.

One of the things about him that makes him so awesome is the way he pays attention to the things I say. He listens. None of the guys I've ever dated before have done that. There was Scott, back in high school. He was a gamer. If I went over to his house, I always had to compete with his system. Kyle was always on his phone. *Always.* Peter had seemed preoccupied most of the time, forever reading something. Anything. If it wasn't a book, or some news article or Wikipedia on his phone, it was the back of cereal boxes.

I'd always felt that I was just an accessory to my boyfriends before, something that just caught their attention briefly, in between other activities. But Jay was interested in hearing about my day, my life in general. Like I say, he wanted to know my whole history, about my absent mom, my dad, my sister. I'd told him about how much I loved Susan, how much she helped me with school, how smart she was. I'd told him how she was always there for me, how she'd looked out for me after my little bout of depression.

I told Jay that it was my turn to feel sorry for Sue now, however. While I was again all happy and in love – I squeezed him – my sister was still *between boyfriends*. She was obviously lonely and out of sorts. I even suggested that this bad mood might've been what had motivated her to accuse him of stealing that money. We had a chuckle about that.

"What kind of guy is she looking for?" he asked me, and I told him that Susan liked 'em tall and thin, built like swimmers. She liked them to be serious and not too talky. She liked them to be not too full of themselves. "And if they're gorgeous, that's definitely a plus."

Jay himself is of course gorgeous, especially so when he smiles. He pulled me onto his lap and kissed my nose. "I think I have just the man for your desperate and dateless sister."

How thoughtful he was, to take the time out of his own life to try to relieve her loneliness. And did she ever once show him any gratitude for it? She most certainly did not.

Try, Try, Try to Understand, He's a Magic Man, Mama

Jay did most of the talking at dinner, because of course, good-looking Jay was a talker. Good-looking Treavor was a listener, I discovered, at least when his buddy was on the mike. What it was Jay discussed, I cannot here relate, however, because I spent the entire meal watching Treavor listening, smiling back when he smiled at me, and overall, ruminating on the possibilities.

The idea that someone as gorgeous as he was couldn't possibly be single didn't enter my mind, because while I didn't often pay too much attention to Bonnie's chirping, the second I saw Jay's roommate, I summoned up all snatches of info that Bonnie had related about him. It wasn't much – she mostly went on and on about the awesome wonderfulness that was Jay, so she hadn't even mentioned that her thief boyfriend's buddy was a blonde Adonis incarnate. How that had slipped her mind, I'll never know. All she'd said was that the two of them lived and worked together, Treavor played the bass, and most importantly, may Heaven rejoice! he was in between girlfriends at the moment.

After dinner, we crowded together on the expensive leather couch and watched a movie, like high school kids. I didn't ask if the couch was new, because another nod to my suspicions of Mr. Right would've just elicited giggles from Bonnie. Fifteen hundred smackers cash American had gone the way of the dodo from our backyard, and while that was certainly unfortunate for her bottom line, the possibility that it could've been none other than the best boyfriend in the world that had stolen it was just high comedy to Bonnie. Hardy har har.

All of the pretty boys' furnishings were fairly new, anyway, stylish and pricey, as, I thought, befitted a bachelor pad inhabited by pretty boys. The place was immaculate, and again, I wondered if they kept it that way themselves or if they had adoring girls in to clean it for them.

When the movie was over, Treavor walked me out to the car, said it was nice to meet me, asked if I'd like to go out with him the following night. Just like that. His request would've been a tad quick, a mite presumptuous, had he not been so devastatingly fine. Just like Jay, I imagined that *No* was not a word with which he was familiar. He mentioned some new band at *The House of Ale* or something equally as pedestrian, but I would've agreed to accompany him to watch paint dry. Since there were more than the requisite number of mirrors in his house, I'm sure he knew I wasn't going to turn him down. Not in this lifetime.

I was surprised but then not really surprised at all to discover that our date was to be double, with Bonnie and Jay. But that was gentlemanly, I supposed. Over the next week, I dined with the three of them every night, Sunday through Thursday, at their place, at Bonnie's new place, switching off with my stepsister for the culinary duties. These perfect boys were not entirely perfect: neither of them could cook, but then, looking like they did, why should they have to?

Bonnie was of course thrilled to have me around, and she cheeped happily about what a cute couple Treavor and I made. It was very pleasant, I must say, feeling that I had a life, friends, maybe even a boyfriend. I even more or less stopped noticing Jay's appraising, inviting stares, as I began to notice (to hope) that Treavor was looking at me the same way.

Over the course of the week, I heard Treavor's life story, although it was mostly Jay that did the telling. They had grown up together; their houses had faced each other across an all-American, tree-lined street, right here in River City. Treavor had two older sisters, who had mothered and coddled him and his dark-haired, only-child playmate. Jay mentioned that the first girl he'd ever kissed had been Treavor's sister Stephanie, but when Bonnie made a face, he hastened to add that it was only a kiss on the cheek. He'd been twelve at the time, and Steph was sixteen – she'd laughed at him.

I would've bet the grocery money that Steph had been the last girl that had ever laughed at his kisses.

Treavor and Jay worked for *Carruthers Brothers' Plumbing*. I smiled at the rhyming title and Treavor smiled at my amusement. "My dad had hoped to rename it *Carruthers and Sons* someday, but my uncle had two daughters and so did he, so it was up to me to scare up a brother to carry on the family tradition. Fortunately, I found one right across the street."

Ah, the admirable bonds of friendship between men! I imagined the two of them in high school, light and dark sides to the same stunning coin, going through the cheerleaders like knives through butter.

"Hey, I know! If we become musicians, we'll get even more action!"

Jay would've done all the talking, while his quieter *brother* just sat there and shook that amazing straight blonde hair out of his eyes, perhaps idly strummed his bass. Treavor's beauty required no clever words. The broken hearts must've been legion.

And now they were doing it again, dating sisters, after a fashion. Bonnie never added the correct appellation of *step,* so neither did Jay or Treavor. After a while, I found that I abandoned it too, in speech if not in thought. Bonnie was too unlike me to really be my sister, and ever since her almost-fatal actions over Peter, I'd thought of her more as a delicate child whose welfare had been entrusted to me. I felt more motherly toward her than sisterly.

Treavor and I went to the movies that Friday, without our chaperones. Apparently there was some other band that Jay wanted to see that Treavor didn't care for. That was the story, anyway. He held my hand, kissed me in the darkness of the theater. Without any surprise at all, I discovered that I *ached* for him. A week had been long enough for propriety, and I longed to loose all the fantasies that had danced through my mind from the second I'd met him.

To my continued delight, Bonnie and Jay were not waiting for us at the big apartment at the foot of the hill, and a quick text to her informed me that they were staying at her place that night. I waited in pluperfect anticipation, every nerve-ending keenly aware, ready, eager for Treavor's touch. I realized that wanting this blondie had occupied the sum of my waking thoughts for the past week.

They were playing an old episode of *Star Trek* in the day room after group today, and in relation to Treavor, I must quote Mr. Spock's words, if only to heartily disagree with them: *After a time, you may find that having is not so pleasing a thing after all as wanting. It is not logical, but it is often true.*

It was not true in this particular case. Wanting Treavor for a week had definitely hurt so good, but having him was infinitely better than merely wanting him. He was what could only be termed as divinely incredible.

Currently, our keepers are screening *Raiders of the Lost Ark* for us. Gotta keep the crazies occupied. Indy just said, *"That thing represents everything we got into archaeology for in the first place,"* and I barked laughter. Angela looked over at me in surprise. Since I've been writing about Treavor, a slight alteration of the line had played through my mind and struck me as hilarious in its apt cleverness: *Treavor Carruthers represented everything I got into heterosexuality for in the first place.*

I scribble this bon mot into my kindergartener's notebook, so Angela'll stop staring at me.

Thinking about Treavor – I may have to go take another shower. I must reiterate that I've always appreciated all the things about men's bodies that are different from my own, and Treavor was all masculine, possessed of those delightful opposites in spades: the broad shoulders, the muscled arms, the powerful chest, the sculpted obliques. And of course, all that glorious blonde hair. The parts that he showed to the world were matched only by the parts that he kept covered. Treavor was my own personal He-Man, and he made me feel like a Master of the Universe, every time he touched me. If you don't get that before-we-were-born reference, Google it.

If anyone ever reads this, I'm sure that the question they'll ask at this point is: Since I was so thoroughly enjoying all that blonde virility on the hoof, did I forget about my redheaded stepbrother and our secret? The answer would be, yes and no. *It's complicated.*

On the glorious level of the physical, if I say that I'd used Peter as my private, local playground (swings and slides!) throughout my teens and early twenties, in comparison, I'd have to say that Treavor was like having Disneyland all to myself. To say that I was happy with my sex life when my stepbrother lived on the other side of the closet from me would've been the grossest of understatements. But I was positively ecstatic with it while I was dating Treavor.

But fortunately or unfortunately, however you choose to look at it, there are more elements to one's interactions with the opposite sex than just sex. And because this is a fact of life, I didn't forget Peter.

The two of us had once been a pair, after a fashion, cut from the same cloth of intellect and temperament. Both of us were introspective, quiet, watchful, and I guess, if I'm honest, both of us had rather a superior streak. That was no doubt the outgrowth of having successfully kept a scandalous relationship on the down-low from the entire world for a long time. Leading a double life made us feel clever.

But I was a part of a quartet now, comprised of three happy, modern people, always up on the latest viral video and Kardashian scandal, and sometimes it was painfully apparent how much I was, and continue to be, not like them. I am proud to say that I've never caught Kim's latest; I've never even heard her speak. That kind of inane popular culture stuff has never interested me.

Sometimes being around my new beau and his friend and my stepsister bored me; sometimes it depressed me. Sometimes, when they would be discussing the latest non-thing – the dress, for example, elicited a two hour discussion – I would say to myself, *Christ! Why do you care? Why would anybody care?*

I was confident that Bonnie looked up to me, felt that I was smarter than her, and of course, I agreed with that estimation, but her superficiality was appalling. She was a follower, of fashion and Facebook and Hollywood gossip. But because she featured herself in love with him, most of all, Bonnie followed Jay.

And that was the main disconcerting characteristic about Treavor, also. Even if I hadn't heard the heartwarming story of boys that lived across the street from each other, it was obvious that they'd grown up together, because Treavor used the same expressions as Jay. He dressed like him. Treavor was two or three months older, but if you didn't know it, you would've thought he was Jay's adoring younger brother, so much did he mimic his friend's words, parrot his opinions.

If the four of us were going out somewhere together, Treavor and Bonnie always waited for Jay to make the decision: we went to the movie Jay wanted to see, ate at the restaurant or drank at the bar Jay chose. We talked about whatever Jay wanted to talk about. If he wasn't present, running his mouth-watering mouth, Bonnie and Treavor talked *about* him, the last funny story he told, how damn witty he was.

My opinion of Jay had not changed, however. Surely, he was startlingly attractive. Whatever else he was, no one could take that away from him. But so was Treavor, and I frequently wondered why their egos and personalities were so dissimilar. Treavor was a nice guy – *Christ save me,* Peter always said, *from being termed a nice guy* – but besides his striking attractiveness, really, there wasn't much else to say about Treavor. He was kind and caring, funny and warm. He was down-to-earth, respectful, happy with his life. He seemed honest. All around, a *nice guy*.

Jay was a son of a bitch, however. All the characteristics that Treavor seemed to come by naturally, *his nice-guyness,* if you will – I thought that Jay was faking all that. He wasn't a nice guy at all. He was a player, a manipulator. Didn't he have his girl and his best friend wrapped around his little finger?

The way he always looked at me, with that appraising, subtle, *Hey, Sue, ya think ya might wanna today?* smile, convinced me that he would betray Bonnie, as well as his best friend, without a single second thought, if I so much as nodded in his direction. I was sure that my lack of interest didn't bother him, didn't keep him honest, however; there were plenty of other girls that nodded at him, that returned that killer smile.

I watched them look at him when we all went out together. They would smile and he would smile, but if they held his gaze for too long, he would immediately enact some PDA with Bonnie: put his arm around her, kiss her cheek, grab her hand. All the while, we would be looking at this other girl. He used Bonnie as a shield, whilst he offered the hopefuls that smug, crooked smile. *I know you want it, baby, but I'm busy with this one right now. How lucky is she? You'll just have to wait your turn. I come in here all the time.*

Just like his apartment, Jay took great care of his car, washing it and detailing it almost weekly. That was no doubt to get rid of the evidence – Jay made sure that Bonnie wouldn't find any lipsticks or *Victoria's Secret* receipts under the seat of his car, even if she'd been smart enough to look for them.

I just knew he wasn't faithful to her. He was *that fast horse;* if the situation was different, I would've tried him out for a few furlongs myself, would've matched him stride for stride. I knew that a stallion like Jay Salteesiak wouldn't run through the paddock with only a My Little Pony like Bonnie exclusively, not when there were so many other sleek fillies, all corralled at *Mickey's,* waiting for him, chomping at the bit.

He was shady, a ladies' man, quite possibly a thief. And if that wasn't enough, he was also illiterate, just like Bonnie and (sadly) Treavor. Not in the modern sense of the word, of course. Mark Twain said, *The man who does not read has no advantage over the man who cannot read,* and that's the sense in which I mean it. They *could* read, but they confined themselves to things of internet-brevity, as befitted their tsetse fly-sized attention spans.

If I ever forgot whose company I was keeping and asked them, "Hey, did you ever read . . .?" The answer was always no, usually followed by a blank look. Not only had they never read it, they'd never even heard of it.

So I wore myself out on Trevor's exquisite body, but if I wanted to exercise my mind, I called Peter. In addition to some refreshing cynicism about the state of the world, he also told me about how his life was going. He was happy that Bonnie was happy, and didn't particularly share my concerns that she was hooked up with the wrong man. Peter was more suspicious about the he-had-to've-done-it-thievery than the idea that Jay was cheating on her.

"Is that insane jealousy thing contagious?" he asked. "Have you caught it, too?" I let the subject drop in the face of his derision.

Peter was amused that I had only swine before which to cast my intellectual pearls; after hearing my laments about Treavor's illiteracy, Peter thereafter referred to him as my *dumb blonde.* He said the beach was still the beach; bright, hot, sandy; too many people, no place to park. He said work was challenging but rewarding, always tiring. He mentioned his roommate-girlfriend not at all. He said he missed me, and despite Treavor, I missed him, too.

But the occasional workout of the little gray cells over the phone with one's intelligent (as well as sexy) stepbrother did not a life make. I was happy enough with my situation, with my shallow, superficial, phenomenal-in-bed boyfriend. I couldn't say that I loved Treavor – although I certainly did love parts of him – but I enjoyed his company, even when we weren't in bed. I didn't have to entertain him; he didn't clamor for my attention every second. If I wanted to read or surf the internet, he played with his game system, or strummed quietly on his bass. He was just *there,* idling, most of the time. But he would flare to life whenever Jay showed up.

Treavor and Bonnie loved Jay, but I wasn't having any. His very presence never failed to cast an oily film of annoyance over my mood. But he wasn't around all the time, nor was chirpy Bonnie. Mostly, it was just Treavor and me, alone at his place, in bed. I missed Peter randomly, but not too much, because Treavor and I alone in bed was really quite awesomely sufficient. After a while it even caused me to quit dwelling upon how much I despised and suspected Jay, at least when I wasn't actually looking at him.

BONNIE'S JOURNAL, PART EIGHT

The perfect man for my dateless sister, or so it turned out, was Jay's roommate and lifetime friend, Treavor Carruthers.

He's cute, but he's shy. He doesn't talk much, but when he does say something, it's always witty and funny. He comes from a big family – two older sisters – and he treats me like I'm the younger sister he never had.

When I started dating Jay, Sue and I ceased to talk about men the way we used to. I'd heard all about her last boyfriend, that George guy from her office, although I never did get to meet him. And I'm sure I bored her (or maybe even embarrassed her) with all the intimate details I told her about her brother. But if I tried to initiate a little girl-talk about Jay, she'd immediately change the subject, as if she'd become a prude or something. Whatever. Mona liked to hear about him.

In light of that behavior, it's funny (but not really funny at all), the things that Susan would say about Jay later.

And Sue never talked to me about Treavor at all, but I was pretty sure that she liked him, regardless, from the things I *heard.* Sometimes, I guess she forgot that Jay and I were just on the other side of the wall (or maybe she just didn't care – Susan was not really in any way a prude). I swear to God, sometimes the squeaking of the bed and her enthusiastic moans could've raised the dead.

"Did I do good, or what?" Jay would say. "Ol' Treav's certainly taken her mind off of giving me dirty looks and telling you I'm a thief."

I had to agree with that.

It was all good times. I saw my sister almost daily – she and Treavor and Jay and I had dinner together nearly every night, either at Jay's place or at mine. Then we parted. I suspected it was because some masculine confab had occurred; perhaps Jay had kidded his friend about his girlfriend being a screamer. We became almost like two married couples. Jay hardly ever stayed at his apartment anymore, and Sue hardly ever stayed at our parents' house. Dad even made a joke about it, that a little lovin' had made Susie go all MIA from the home fires. Having had more than his share of lovin' in his life, Dad always pointed out such things about people, made jokes about them. He embarrassed me in this case, by hitting the nail directly on the head.

Yeah, Susan seemed happy with Treavor. She was too busy with what they did behind closed doors to do much of anything else, actually. But the calm before the crazy-storm would last for only about six or seven months.

Her and Bobby Were Steppin' Out,
Her and Bobby Didn't Know I Found Out.
Do Ya Know What I Mean?

(I guess the oldies are growing on me. Or maybe it's the medication.)

My idyllic (if somewhat intellectually bankrupt) life proceeded, *shorter of breath and one day closer to death,* for about six months. My world revolved around Treavor; Bonnie and Jay orbited nearby, not close enough to be unbearably annoying, and Peter sent me texted communiques from Beachworld, located in a galaxy far, far, away. Perhaps I would've carried on in this manner indefinitely; what else did I have to do?

Then I observed something that was unique in my experience. I'd never seen such a thing firsthand, even though I was not unaware that it existed. It happened thus:

It was a Saturday morning. I had of course spent the night at Treavor's, whilst Bonnie, the Happy Hausfrau, had kept what she thought was her devoted husband at her place. My blondie was an early riser, and while he wasn't much of a cook, he could whip up a mean stack of pancakes. So I lingered in bed after he got up, sated, smug. Hot damn, he was good!

Eventually, the inviting smells of breakfast on its way roused me. I got dressed, went out to greet the new day the Lord had made. But when I turned the corner into the hall, I almost ran smack into the most curious thing.

There was a short expanse of wall perpendicular to the front door, directly in my line of sight, so it wasn't like there were any obstructions, that I could've mis-seen somehow. I can claim to be an absolutely certain eyewitness. What I saw, and its implications, was utterly clear to me.

Jay had his back against the wall. Treavor had his hands on either side of Jay's shoulders, palms flat against the same wall. If either would've turned his head toward the hallway, they would've seen me standing there. Jay rested his forearms on Treavor's shoulders, gestured idly with his hands behind Treavor's head, while they smiled and spoke in soft voices.

Surely, it wasn't some kind of torrid clutch, but I saw it all in a flash, nonetheless. This was not a posture your average pair of buddies assumed. One step forward, a bending of the elbows, and Treavor, obviously the aggressor, would've had Jay pinned to the wall. One tiny step, and Jay's arms would've slid the rest of the way around Treavor's neck. And then it *would've* been a torrid clutch.

'Tis so strange, that, though the truth of it stands off as gross as black and white, my eye will scarcely see it. Irresistible Jay and incredible Treavor were lovers, and even more contrary, more unlikely than that, like I say, Treavor was the aggressor. All that deferring to Jay's decisions, listening to him talk, copying his clothes and mannerisms – those actions occurred in another ring of the circus. Here, in the center ring, it was Treavor calling the shots. Here, Jay was *his* pet.

They whispered for another second, and it gave me time to stop and consider this never-dreamt-of turn of events. There was not one single thing effeminate about either of them, so who woulda thunk it? From Bonnie's rosy reports and my own delightful experiences, the thought that Jay and Treavor might've played for both teams had never, *ever* crossed my mind. But on the other hand, what did I know about these kinds of things? Absolutely nothing, that's what.

But it was obviously true, regardless. Men that were not *exceptionally* well acquainted didn't stand this close to each other. One didn't put his arms on the other one's shoulders. The other one didn't allow it, not even if they were childhood buddies, not even if they actually *were* brothers.

That word, *brothers,* brought Peter to mind, and I saw my situation with him reflected back to me from across the room. The mirror was clear, the distortion minimal.

As teenagers, Peter and I had each had the unspeakably good fortune to discover a safe, utterly enjoyable, infinitely convenient lover right on the other side of the closet. But because of the taboos – we were just kids; we were supposed to be brother and sister – we'd kept it a secret. We'd grown up, matured, dated others. But still our secret remained, even if we hadn't taken advantage of it lately. I now kenned that a similar situation existed between Treavor and Jay.

Perhaps some night when they were boys, camping out in the backyard, the flashlights and ghost stories had suddenly been forgotten. Maybe they'd discovered this new activity, *discovered each other,* just as Peter and I had done. And just like us, because they liked it, they'd kept it up, through maturity and dating women. But such proclivities carried their own taboos, and – I couldn't know for sure of course, but seeing as how they were both consummate with the opposite sex – I suspected that maybe they were only queer for each other. Maybe that's why they'd kept it a secret. Who knows how these kind of things work? Certainly not I.

But one thing was certain: they were definitely more than just buddies. Or perhaps it could be said that they were indeed *the very best* of buddies, just like Peter and me.

I stepped silently back into the bedroom to allow them to have their moment. I waited for an angry feeling of betrayal to manifest, but wasn't surprised at all when it didn't. True: the idea that my boyfriend and Bonnie's boyfriend were secretly lovers cast some shade on nice-guy Treavor. But it was par for the course as far as my opinion of Jay went. I'd always believed that he'd fuck anything that walked, and the discovery that this included his best friend, surprised me not at all.

But while I may be a lot of things, a hypocrite isn't one of them. How could I feel angry or betrayed that my boyfriend might still be sharing more than just a *How the hell are ya?* with Jay, his lifelong pal? If I'd had the opportunity to see

Peter over the past several months, we would've, beyond a shadow of a doubt, renewed our old friendship in the bitchin' old ways. Having Treavor, and Peter, as well – I wouldn't have hesitated. I would've been the epitome, the very dictionary illustration of *having my cake and eating it, too.* Life is short.

My thing with my stepbrother had existed before my thing with Treavor; one had nothing whatsoever to do with the other. Treavor and Jay's thing had obviously existed for quite some time, and it certainly had nothing to do with me, so how could I possibly care? It wasn't as if I loved Treavor; it wasn't as if I imagined some kind of happily ever after with him. And it wasn't as if Jay, his *brother,* was another woman, now was it? I didn't mind sharing Treavor with this preexisting, different-from-me condition.

But Bonnie . . . Well, Bonnie just wouldn't understand. Just like my thing with Peter could not've been construed as any kind of conscious betrayal of Bonnie, I had to cut Sleazy Salteesiak some slack this time. He and Treavor – just like me and Peter – it wasn't any of Bonnie's bidness. Nor was it any of mine. It didn't have anything to do with either of us.

Bonnie would never believe such a totally unexpected thing, anyway, just like she refused to believe that Mr. Wonderful had pocketed her rent money. If I let this cat out of the bag, it would surely cause them to break up, and while it was certainly true that I would've dearly loved to see Bonnie and Jay break up, I'd just have to accomplish it through other means. If I told her about this, I'd only be hurting myself. I would be hoist on my own petard. Outing Treavor and Jay to Bonnie would cut me off from Treavor's awesomeness, and I wasn't going to sacrifice my own enjoyment just because Bonnie was too stupid to see that she'd hooked up with someone who was clearly too much man for her. If the situation was reversed, she surely wouldn't have sacrificed her enjoyment for me.

"Treavor?" I called from the bedroom. "Are you making breakfast?" It was lame and I knew it, but it gave them fair warning that I was coming out. They were still standing in front of the door, but now there was plenty of room for Jesus in between them: they were standing as befitted two heterosexual men.

I feigned surprise at Jay's presence, asked him where Bonnie was, because hey, hey, what d'ya know, I was quite sure she wasn't there. He said she'd been struck with a case of tummy troubles the night before, so he'd come on home to leave her in peace.

I knew, therefore, that he'd arrived after Treavor and I had retired, that he'd been there all night. And his crooked grin told me that not only had he heard my sometimes vociferously vocal responses to my boyfriend's caresses, he wanted me *to know* that he'd heard them. That Jay was an auditory voyeur didn't subtract much more from the low opinion I already held of him. And thinking about what I'd just seen, the sudden realization that he and Treavor no doubt compared notes – Peter and I discussed our other lovers with each other – this idea didn't bother me in the least. Men talked, women talked, lovers talked; I was confident that Treavor's reports on my performance were glowing.

I called Bonnie to inquire how she was feeling, and when she said, "Sick as a dog," I immediately said, "You're not–"

"No, I'm not." She paused, then added, "But I don't think it would be such a bad thing. I love Jay and he loves me–"

"Christ, Bonnie! You're not trying, are you?"

I felt like I'd suddenly been thrust into *The Twilight Zone*. I imagined that house and picket fence, with two cats in the yard and maybe two or three blue-eyed babies, and Uncle Treavor always there, hovering. Sure, it was his and Jay's secret, and they were entitled to it, but if Bonnie ever found out, and if she'd already had a couple of kids when she did . . . Yikes!

"No, I'm not trying. Are you insane? I don't want any kids right now. I'm just saying, if I was, it would be okay, I guess. But I'm not. It's some kind of food poisoning."

I asked her if they'd eaten at *Mickey's* the night before, and when she said they had, I wrote that mystery off as solved right there. I'd often joked that the Health Department *A* in their window was short for *A Case of Ptomaine Waiting to Happen.* Hardy har har. I slay me.

I asked Bonnie if she needed any Pepto or anything, and she said she was set, was in fact feeling better already. She told me to text her later.

Treavor and Jay were waiting for me to get off the phone. I sat down at the kitchen table and we tucked into Blondie's excellent pancakes. Through the prism of what I'd glimpsed of their true relationship, I marveled at how domestic they were. I wondered if Peter and I would've been like this, had we ever gotten the opportunity to live together: happy halves to a whole, lovers when we were alone together, players on the world stage with other actors, otherwise.

I noticed that Jay was wearing a work shirt: the three letters of his anonymous, straight-out-of-a-porno name were cartouched in an oval above one pocket, and *Carruthers' Brothers Plumbing* was embroidered above the other. He noticed me noticing, and said that since Bonnie was feeling under the weather, he'd decided to pick up some overtime. As if I cared in the slightest what he would be doing with his day. Treavor told him good luck with all that – his check was gonna be fine this week.

Ruminating on what I'd almost walked in on earlier, coupled with the idea that Jay's very *name* had always put be in mind of a character in a dirty movie, I wondered vaguely if they ever sometimes worked on the same jobs together, if they ever actually went out in the same truck on calls, like some kind of plumberly dynamic duo. Did they ever *service* some lucky lady at the same time? I shivered quite involuntarily at the thought of that.

Treavor was telling Jay that he definitely had plans other than working today, and his smile told me that they didn't involve leaving his apartment. Jay offered me an *Atta girl!* wink, then was soon gone, thank Christ, taking my thoughts of *both of them at the same time* out the door with him. It had been just a passing fancy – even if there was no Bonnie, it wasn't something that I would ever actually pursue in the real world. Treavor was enough for me, right? And I didn't even *like* Jay.

(The voice of a slutty friend from high school points out that I'm lying to myself. "I don't have to like 'em, I just have to like what they do." And the thought of *both of them* . . . Mercy.)

All good things must come to an end, however, even lovely mornings in bed with my exquisite blondie. Since he'd made breakfast, I volunteered to make lunch, but when I went out to the kitchen, Mother Hubbard, I discovered that the cupboard was mostly bare. I told him to take a little nap, to rest up for Round Two, whilst I went to the store to pick up a few groceries.

I drove through the quiet residential streets that led up the hill to the more main thoroughfare, upon which the market sat. At a stop sign, I happened to see a *Carruthers' Brothers Plumbing* truck parked up ahead, on the right. I knew it was Jay's, because I'd seen it before: on the back bumper, there was a small smiley face sticker with a bloody bullet hole between its blank eyes. It was faded, barely noticeable; I figured perhaps that was why Treavor's dad hadn't made him scrape off the offensive thing. Or maybe all the trucks had identifying stickers: on the same place on the bumper, Treavor's truck had an old-fashioned peace sign.

I went on to the store, picked up staples for a hearty, now-getting-onto-late lunch, and something for dinner. When I was on my way back, Jay's truck was still there. Before I passed it, before I'd even had time to move off from the stop sign, I saw him come out of the house.

I'd been amused with Jay and Treavor's secret, had been feeling a kind of empathy with them – we all had our peccadillos, and it turned out that they were quite similar, were they not? The other thing I'd mused about, the glories of a ménage a trois with these *very good buddies* – that had even further faded my dislike and distrust of my stepsister's boyfriend.

But only for a minute. It's said that everything happens for a reason, and what I witnessed next narrowed my perceptions back to where they should've been. It served to whet my almost blunted purpose. Jay Salteesiak was a son of a bitch, and come hell or high water, Bonnie had to be convinced of that.

And now I had him. He was busted.

Jay had his arm around the shoulders of a pretty blonde woman, about our age, and she had her arm, familiarly, possessively, around his waist. Fortunately, no one had come up behind me at the stop sign, so I fumbled my phone out of my purse, and like a good private eye, I took pictures.

Jay gave her a companionable hug, then kissed her on the forehead. The girl – she was exceptionally lovely, with stunning, white-blonde hair – she squeezed him right on back. And I got it all on my phone, click, click, click. Evidence.

While Jay was still talking to her, I breezed on through the stop sign. Too busy with his little-on-the-side, he didn't even notice my car.

I ran the groceries quickly up to Treavor's apartment, and as luck would have it, he was indeed napping, so I didn't even have to make up some excuse to go see Bonnie.

She thought she'd caught Peter's infidelity, based on an ownerless tube of lipstick and an equally ownerless nightie? That was all circumstantial, at best; items in his vicinity that belonged to women didn't necessarily place the women themselves in the kip with him. But I'd caught Jay in the act, hugging and kissing on a living, breathing female, a beautiful blonde.

"It's better that you found out sooner rather than later," I'd tell Bonnie, with a sad, pitying expression. I'd comfort her, hand her tissues for her tears, make sure that there was no repeat of the maudlin histrionics of the last time. And after the storm of her betrayal blew itself out – I probably wouldn't be having too many dinners with Jay anymore, hee, hee. Good riddance.

But there was absolutely nothing to stop me from still seeing Treavor. Maybe I'd have to invest in my own love nest to entertain him, but maybe it was about time for that, too.

BONNIE'S JOURNAL, PART NINE

The first time Susan came to me with her craziness about Jay, the scene played out like some kind of weepy old movie. (Maybe I should count it as the second time; the first instance of insanity was her totally off-the-wall accusation that he'd stolen my money.)

I'd eaten something bad the night before, and Jay said that he was going to pick up a few hours at work, and let me rest. He knew that I was short on funds, because I was still paying Jon and my dad back the money I owed them, so he'd been gracious enough to've been putting food on the table for our entire relationship. Now he was going out to earn some more. Was that something a thief would do?

I was sitting on the couch when Susan knocked. I told her to come in, and to my surprise, she sat down right next to me, took my hand. Just like in some tragic play, her actions immediately worried me, because Sue was never the physically demonstrative type, at least not with me. She was always hanging all over Treavor, but she seldom gave me as much as a pat on the back. But on the other hand, her words had always been comfort enough.

"I've got some bad news, Bonnie," she said, scaring me already. "I don't really know how to say it, so I'll say it quickly, like ripping off a Band-Aid. Jay is—"

"Something's happened to Jay?" I cried, and squeezed her hand. All that was missing was some mournful tune playing in the background. The fear coursed through me like a painful electric shock. I wouldn't have to kill myself if Jay was gone. I'd just die from grief.

"No, honey. Nothing's happened to him. I just saw him, actually." Susan took a deep breath, slowly let it out. "Jay's cheating on you, Bonnie."

I was dumbfounded by her statement, didn't even have the voice to say, *"What?"* because now the conflicting emotions struggled to sort themselves out. Susan's solemn expression, *I've got some bad news.* Oh, my God, Jay's dead! Jay's not dead, he's okay, but now some sounds, senseless vowels and consonants from Susan, something that sounded like *Jay's cheating on you.* Relief that he was not dead mixed with disbelief. I was speechless.

So Sue took her phone out of her purse, still all grave and gloomy, and handed it to me. I didn't want to take it, because now other feelings warred in me. The sour, stomach-roiling bitterness I'd felt at the idea of that bastard Peter with some other girl, fought, hand to hand, with the portrait of Jay's smiling face, so clear in my mind.

Jay wasn't like Peter. He loved me and I loved him and he would never cheat on me. He wasn't like Peter, and he knew how much Peter had hurt me. But Susan loved me, too, also knew how much Peter had hurt me, and if she was saying that Jay was cheating on me, shoving her phone into my hands . . . I didn't want to see. But I had to see. If it was true, I had to know.

The nausea from the night before returned, much worse because of what Sue was telling me. It was like some big gorilla-hand was squeezing my guts. I knew that I was gonna throw up again; I wouldn't be able to stop it. But I had enough control – I had to see first.

I took a deep breath, held it. I felt so sick that I thought I might pass out, but I swiped the screen. There were probably twenty pics, taken in quick succession, like some kind of fashion shoot. Going through them, it was like they were animated. Jay hugging a girl, kissing her forehead; the girl smiling at him, hugging him back. All the famous sayings played through my head: Susan had Jay *dead to rights* with these pictures, they were *the smoking gun.* Just like Peter had been, the best boyfriend in the world had been *caught red-handed.*

Except . . .

The nausea lifted and was gone in a heartbeat. I smiled at Sue, then I giggled. The giggle grew into a big belly laugh, and I just let it out. I wasn't like I could've stopped it.

Susan was alarmed at my unexpected reaction. From the look on her face, she thought I'd lost my marbles. Here was Jay, *apprehended with the goods,* you might say – and I wasn't sobbing and looking for the pill bottle, like Sue had expected me to do. The tears were running down my face, but they were from laughter.

This reaction freaked her out, and she said, "Oh, honey, I'm so sorry! But it's gonna be okay!" She even clumsily put her hand on my shoulder.

"Yeah, it's gonna be okay," I told her. I handed her phone back and another titter escaped. "Do you find anything at all familiar about that girl? Anything at all?"

"She's very pretty," Sue replied. Then realizing that probably wasn't the best thing to say, she added quickly, "But I've never seen her before in my life."

"Does she remind you of anyone, though?" I insisted.

Susan wasn't looking at her phone. She was searching my face, wondering just what the hell was wrong with me, that I wasn't sobbing at Jay's betrayal. She repeated, "I don't know her, Bonnie, and what possible difference could it make–"

"That's Treavor's sister, Sue."

Now she studied the pic, and now that she knew, I'm sure the family resemblance struck her as undeniable. She looked back up at me, but the relief I expected to see on her face wasn't there.

"That's Stephanie?"

"No, that's Marilyn." Susan continued to look shocked, and I giggled again. "She's a year younger than Steph. Steph lives up in Canyon Crest now. She's a doctor. Her husband's a surgeon–"

"When did you ever meet–"

"I went to dinner at Treavor's parents' house, before you met him. The whole tribe was there. Jay's like a part of their family, so he wanted to show me off to them."

"I don't see how the fact that she's Treavor's sister makes a damn bit of difference," Susan said with grim anger. She gestured with her phone. "Jay kissed her."

"He kissed her on the forehead. He's like another brother to her. She's married, Sue. She's got two young kids."

"Maybe they're Jay's," Sue replied, and I blinked in surprise at the disgusting implication. "Christ, Bonnie! How can you be so blind? Just because she's married and he's seeing you, doesn't mean they're not–"

"This just happened, huh?" I asked her calmly. "It wasn't hours ago, or yesterday, was it? You know how I know that? Marilyn called me. Asked me to thank Jay again for coming right out. She said her dad always puts family plumbing problems on the back burner, but Jay came right out–"

"She called you because they were already done."

Again, I was shocked at how her vulgar little mind worked. But still I didn't foresee any trouble coming.

Susan knew what she thought she'd seen, and she was doing her sisterly duty to report it to me. Although, I did think that if she was really looking out for me, she should've talked to Jay first. She should've demanded an explanation from him before she came over here and got my stomach all shook up with her baseless accusations, like in some tearful Lifetime movie. He would've told her that the girl was Treavor's sister, that they were old friends, and that would've been the end of it. Or, if Susan was still suspicious, if she still felt that she had to tattle on Jay, it would've been not at all as stressful and jarring if she would've known ahead of time, if she would've been able to say, "I saw Jay with Treavor's sister and I think something's going on."

"If Marilyn and Jay are having an affair, why would she bother calling me at all?" I asked my over-protective sister. I remembered her other accusation and said, "I know you still think he took that money."

"It couldn't't've been anyone *but* him."

She was like a parrot on that. *Jay's a thief! Jay's a thief! AWWK!*

"Whatever." I could show annoyance, too, just like she and Peter did. "Jay didn't rob me, and he's not cheating on me, Sue. Come back when you've got pictures of him with his arm around someone besides his best friend's sister. Someone he hasn't known all his life."

"You're just dumb, Bonnie, you know that?" she told me coldly.

I'm sorry to say I did it, but I just looked pointedly at the door, then. Maybe I should've thanked her for looking out for me. Maybe I should've asked her why she suspected Jay so much, all the time, and then maybe it would've all come out then, instead of building up into a burst of insanity. But I didn't ask her anything. I just looked at the door, and she got the hint.

Susan crossed the room, but before she left, she said, "Don't tell him I saw him."

"Why not? I think it's funny, and I'm sure he will, too. And Treavor–"

"I'm asking you, Bonnie," she said emphatically. *"Don't tell Jay I saw him."*

"Oh, all right."

I thought that Sue had realized her error, and didn't want Jay and the whole Carruthers family laughing at her. But maybe that wasn't it at all.

Paging Doctor Freud

Angela tried to kill herself this morning.

Where there's a will, as the old saying goes, a way will be found. She didn't try to do it all at once. Before group, she must've tied the sheet to the closet pole, then afterwards, she just looped it around her neck, knelt over, and jerked herself forward. I don't know how effective it would've been, but I guess she figured fifteen minutes would've been long enough. But when I saw that her door was closed – the staff frowned on that – maybe I had a premonition. I knocked, went in; I screamed, and they took her out of here. Probably to a more secure place. A padded cell, maybe, if they still have those. Or maybe they'll just dope her up. No more straitjackets, nowadays. They call it *chemical restraint* in the brave new Snake Pit.

What with the hurried running through the halls, and the hauling away of poor, dumb Angela on a gurney, the rest of the patients guessed what had occurred. I thought that the staff might've held some kind of emergency group or something, to calm us down, to assure us, but better than that, I finally got to see a doctor. A Ph, by God, D.

Today is the third day I've been here, not counting the first evening, when I was brought in. I mostly slept through that. I've coasted all this time, taking my medication, sitting in the day room, watching television, writing my confessions, blending with the other nuts. I've gone to group therapy sessions with counselors, twice a day. They encourage us to talk about what got us here, but I haven't said anything. I feel as though my situation isn't the business of any of the suicidal housewives and depressed hipsters in here with me. Besides, who are these mere counselors to shrink *me?* They're persistent and soft spoken, they seem kind; but whatever else they are, they aren't PhDs. It was high time, as the saying goes, that I got my turn with a professional.

Because I didn't attend college, I have both an odd respect and a plain old resentment for those that have. I'm a trifle ashamed of myself that I never went, and I admire all the hard work and stick-to-it-ive-ness that earned the graduates those initials after their names. On the other hand, that doesn't make them smarter than me.

And as far as shrinks go, well . . . I don't know a whole lot about psychology, so I figured that this guy was gonna be sneaky. He was gonna try to trick me into revealing things that I wanted to keep to myself, lead me to let certain cats out of their bags, release pigs from their pokes – all issues that had no bearing whatsoever on goddamned Jay. I felt intelligent enough to be wary, but uneducated enough to be afraid that the doctor was going to lead me onto paths that I'd just as soon bypass. To continue with the mental health profession theme, you might say I was a quite a bit *paranoid* about that.

His name was Dr. Crowell. I estimated him to be fiftyish or so. He was graying, chubby, bespectacled. He wore a thick, plain, gold wedding band. All around, he looked like a shrink. He introduced himself, offered his hand, and I shook it. It struck me as unfair that he had a file on me – he took a moment to peruse it – so he knew everything about me, whilst I had to guess about him.

He apologized that he hadn't had a chance to see me before now. I replied that it was okay, that I was sure that he was busy. I told him that it wasn't like I was suicidal like Angela, that I needed immediate shrinking.

He smiled at my wit, thanked me for my patience. Then he asked, "How are you feeling today?"

A fair opening gambit, but it could go any number of ways, now couldn't it? I thought of *Raiders* again, and the menacing German: *Now, what shall we talk about?*

"I'm okay. I'm a little worried about Angela."

"I understand that you found her?"

I nodded.

"And she's your friend? How do you feel about what she did?"

"I feel sorry for her. The whole reason she's here – she's got herself all worked up because her husband left her. I want to tell her, men are like buses. There'll be another one along in a minute."

How's that for some blithe philosophy, Dr. Freud? How am I feeling today? Why, I'm just peachy.

"Maybe her husband is special to her. Maybe she doesn't want another man."

"Well, you know what they say. Want in one hand . . . The Stones put it best. *You can't always get what you want.*"

Dr. Crowell scribbled something, and I watched the second hand on the wall clock behind his head. At this rate, the hour, or however long I was gonna be in there, would whiz right on by.

"Are you married, Susan?"

You know I'm not, Doc. I'm sure it says so, right there in my file. But I thought we didn't have to dance around my marital status. That was safe enough territory.

"No. But I do have a boyfriend. His name's Treavor."

Dr. Crowell glanced at my file again. "I see your sister also has a boyfriend."

I smirked. "Unfortunately."

His eyebrows, bushy, went up. "You don't care for your sister's boyfriend?"

"I think that's obvious."

How cool was I? I didn't correct him, didn't say that Bonnie wasn't my sister at all. That might've indicated that there was some kind of animosity between us, which certainly isn't the case. And there was no point in denying my dislike of Jay. My actions on that score were what had landed me here, and the good doctor knew it.

He wanted to talk about that conniving bastard? I was ready.

But Dr. Crowell went in another direction. "Tell me about the rest of your family. Your sister – she's two years younger than you? I see you have a brother, too?"

"A stepbrother."

Here was the minefield, where I feared college-educated, shrink trickery on his part, inadvertent Freudian slips on mine. I was already in the booby hatch, and spilling the beans about my incestuous relationship with Peter might just keep me here. What we did, what we'd been doing for years – it just wasn't done in polite society. The things we shared – for the appearance of cultural normalcy, those cats and pigs needed to stay in their sacks.

Dr. Crowell shook his head. "I'm sorry, Susan. Our intake people – it just says brother and sister. I talked to your sister."

My expression gave away my surprise, but I was cool enough not to speak, not to demand to know what she'd said.

"She's very concerned about you."

I didn't comment on Bonnie's concern, but if she'd called him, then she'd undoubtedly explained to him our exact sibling status. So if I didn't clarify, why, it might look like I was hiding something.

"Bonnie's actually my stepsister, Doctor. Just like my stepbrother – we're all only related by marriage."

"Has your stepbrother been in to visit you?"

Ah, no, Dr. Freud, you're not going to get some flare-up of better-kept-unsaid emotion over that one. The truth: "He probably doesn't even know I'm here." And the untruth: "We've never been that close."

"Wouldn't your sister have told him?"

"They don't really talk."

"Why is that?"

Wasn't this supposed to be my therapy? Why did he care about my by-marriage siblings? But this was also safe ground, and the minutes were ticking past, so I told him, "They had a relationship. It didn't work out."

111

The eyebrows went up. "A sexual relationship?"

"Bonnie was twenty when her dad married my mom. Peter's dad was my mom's second husband; he's passed on. Bonnie never thought of Peter as her brother – she only lived with us for a short time, then moved out so she could date him."

"But it didn't work out?"

I pictured Bonnie, the very embodiment of TMI: *Oh, Doctor, I was so distraught, I tried to kill myself! Susan saved me. She helped me through the aftermath, and now . . . Oh, Doctor, why is this happening?*

Dr. Crowell was fishing for something. I didn't know what it was, but time was almost up, so I reiterated what Bonnie had no doubt already told him.

"Bonnie thought Peter was cheating on her. She tried to kill herself. Her father threw him out, and he moved to the beach. They haven't spoken since."

"Was he cheating on her?"

I shrugged, elaborately noncommittal. "I don't think he was. He said he wasn't."

"But you've told Bonnie that her boyfriend is cheating on her."

So asking about the fortunately canceled-with-no-reruns *Peter and Bonnie Show* had been Dr. Crowell's roundabout path to the matter at hand. That was all good. I didn't mind talking about Jay, if it would mean we would leave off talking about Peter.

"I saw him with other women."

The phone buzzed on the doctor's desk. "I'm sorry, Susan. I have to take this. We'll talk again soon."

I was dismissed. I thought it best to jot down here what the doctor and I had discussed, so as to be better prepared for our next session. *What's past is prologue,* and all. He'll undoubtedly want to talk about what happened with Jay when next we meet, and I want to be sure to have my story straight.

I Met a German Girl in England Who Was Goin' to School in France, Said We Danced the Mississippi at an Alpha Kappa Dance – It Wasn't Me

In further preparation for my next talk with my doctor, I think I'll get my proofs that Jay is a son of a bitch in order. Line those ducks up, so to speak.

First, a jury of his peers would've handed down the obvious verdict: he's a thief.

Then, there's the fact that he's way too chummy with Treavor's sister. Bonnie had dismissed the photographic evidence of that, wrote it off as the two of them being just affectionate old friends. But I knew something that she didn't: Jay was also damn affectionate with Treavor, another of his old friends. Maybe he's some kind of shared paramour with all the Carruthers' siblings, brother and sisters. It would not surprise me in the least.

Bonnie laughed off Jay and Marilyn, so I amassed other proofs of his perfidy, other examples that he was cheating on her.

It was just getting dark one evening, and under the cover of seeling night, Jay didn't see me as I pulled up a few spaces behind him on the street in front of his apartment. He was facing away from me, behind his car; he was putting his *axe* and a small practice amp into the trunk.

Just where was Mr. Wonderful going with that instrument that only added to his attractiveness? Where was his wifely girlfriend? These were legitimate questions for a concerned stepsister to ask. So I followed him.

When he pulled up in front of a brightly lit old Victorian – sadly, it had seen better days: the paint was dull and it had been cut up into several apartments – I knew Jay's alleged errand. I remembered: it was Tuesday, and Bonnie had a late class on Tuesdays, enabling Jay to escape her clutches. He gave guitar lessons on Tuesdays. That was the story, anyway.

As he extracted his instrument and amp from his trunk, the girl came out of the house, down the steps. She just couldn't wait to see him! She was carrying a guitar of her own, a garish, red Flying V, which she held up for his perusal. Jay smiled at it, smiled at her; I snapped a picture of them just before they turned and went on into the house. Jay didn't put his arm around her, because his hands were full. But I was confident that he would've, otherwise. She was quite the sexy student, about twenty-two, tall, willowy, pale, dressed in tight black leather. She had her jet black hair cut in a fair imitation of Davey Havok, short on one side of the part, hanging long and in her eyes on the other. She had a tattoo on her neck; she wore bright red lipstick. She had a multitude of bangles on her wrists, many rings on her fingers and in her ears and nose.

Jay's wild and sensual punk princess was a far cry from backward and homey Bonnie. I figured that it wouldn't be long before the two of them forgot about scales and notes and frets in favor of more enjoyable rock and roll style pursuits. As the saying goes, guitar players do it best.

Before I had a chance to pull away from the curb, Treavor sent me a text: *?* He was a man of few words. I realized that I was late for dinner – right, we were gonna have it alone tonight, because Bonnie was at school and Jay was on the boulevard, giving lessons. I texted back that I would be right there, and hurried home to his place. Treavor had probably bought Chinese – he'd have chopsticks and fortune cookies. And then later . . . Telling Bonnie about what Jay was really teaching would have to be postponed until the morrow.

Wednesday and Thursday passed; I didn't get a chance to break the sad but not unexpected news to my stepsister. I just couldn't carve out a sufficient time alone with her. But then luck smiled on me in another way.

The four of us had gathered immediately after work. It was my turn to prepare the Friday feast, and I was looking at my phone for recipes. I suggested a nice baked chicken parmesan; as one, Bonnie and Treavor looked over at Jay for his opinion.

He was also on his phone, but then glanced up at his adoring fans. "That takes a minute, right?"

"A few," I replied.

"That sounds great, then. Mom just asked me to do her a favor. I won't be gone more than forty-five minute or so."

Needless to say, alarm bells went off in my head. I didn't believe his Blue-eyed Majesty was such a good son that he'd just drop everything and answer his mama's summons, before dinner on a Friday night. My suspicions were further heightened when he picked his guitar up off its stand. Did Mom need a serenade?

But trusting Bonnie was oblivious. Jay walked over to the door with her, murmured a couple of words and kissed her goodbye.

"Shit," I said to neither of my remaining companions particularly. "It says I need egg for this. I'll be right back." Before either of them had time to comment, to check to see if we already had eggs, I grabbed my purse and was gone, like the oft-mentioned wind.

I spotted Jay's taillights at the end of the block, and just had time to hop in the car and follow him.

The front porch of this house wasn't as brightly lit as the punk princess's, but I could still see that the woman who opened the door wasn't anyone that could've possibly been mistaken for Jay's mom. She wasn't old enough; probably only in her mid-thirties. She smiled at him, and then a second girl, probably about twentyish – I couldn't accurately tell, because the porch was dim – appeared beside her and gave Jay a big hug. The first woman took his guitar, and Jay proceeded into the house, carrying his small amp, the other arm wrapped around the second girl's shoulders.

115

The memory of my own sexy guitarist played through my mind, his smile and killer licks. The old Pat Travers cover that was one of his band's staples described Jay to a T: *You're like a bad rumor, baby. You're all over town.*

Guitar lessons. Right. What a novel excuse. I was sure Jay was giving them all something, two at a time, this time, and he might indeed be instructing them. But his schooling didn't have anything to do with his *axe.*

BONNIE'S JOURNAL, PART TEN

Susan's laughable accusations about Jay and Treavor's sister were just the beginning.

On a Saturday morning, one of the rare ones where we were all under the same roof at Jay's place, while he and Treavor were still asleep, Susan hauled out the old cellphone again. She trotted out the same misguided accusation: Jay was cheating on me. He wasn't teaching guitar at all. He was carrying on multiple affairs.

She showed me some nice clear pictures of a tall girl with a weird haircut. I recognized her immediately from Jay's description.

Then she showed me a few dim, grainy shots of two other girls. I recognized them, too, from what Jay had told me. Susan was so wrong about him. He wasn't shady, he wasn't a thief. He always let me know where he was going, and he certainly wasn't cheating on me.

I sighed in annoyance. Really, this was just getting to be too much. "The first one – that must be Alicia. Jay says she wants to be the next big rock star. Has a band and everything, already. Only problem is, she doesn't know how to play."

"I'm sure she knows how to play with him."

Jesus, she was so crude!

"Jay's not her type, Sue. She's a lesbian."

The shocked look on her face was hilarious.

"And the other ones – that was last night, huh?"

She nodded, with her mouth still hanging open.

"Well, yeah, then. You're partially right. The younger girl – she's got a huge crush on Jay. That's for sure."

"So how can you be so calm–"

"His mom called, remember? She works with the older girl. Carrie or Karen or something. The younger one – that's her sister. Karen and her husband and her sister met Jay at his mom's company picnic. The little girl was quite taken with him."

"She's not a little girl, Bonnie."

"Not to look at her. But she's handicapped, Sue. Jay told me she has a mental age of about eight. She liked him so much when they met, so he promised her he'd give her a couple lessons. He was just being nice at the time, but then his mom called last night, said Karen asked if he might have a few minutes. So he went. He keeps his promises."

I gave Sue's phone back to her, and studied her curiously. "Are you following Jay?"

She said that it was all coincidence, that she'd just *happened* to see his truck in front of Marilyn's, his car outside of Alicia's; that she'd passed him going to the store last night, when he was at Karen's. But every time, she'd taken pictures, so in thinking about it now, she must've been following him. I should've noticed then that she'd become way too entirely concerned with him. Obsessed, one might even say. But at the time, I just put it down to protectiveness, to one sister looking out for another.

Nowadays . . . I don't think it was that any more.

Laugh About It, Shout About It, When You've Got To Choose,
Every Way You Look at This You Lose

The nurse told me that Dr. Crowell will see me again tomorrow, right after group. I'm wondering about how he's gonna conduct his analysis. But I'm ready to talk, I guess, at least about Jay. I'm kind of getting tired of being in here. Hopefully, Treavor or Bonnie called my office, made up some excuse for my no-call, no-show absence. I've got Ebola, maybe. If not, well . . . I was looking for a job when I found that one. It's not like I've got rent to pay.

Once I tell my story, and the doctor understands how it happened, I'm sure he'll let me go home. Maybe I overreacted a bit – that's why they put me in here. But after I talk to Dr. Crowell, he'll see that I'm calm now, that I'm not likely to do it again. They'll see that I'm right about Jay. Bonnie'll see, too. She'll dump him, get on with her life. She'll find somebody new, somebody maybe not so cute, but more loyal.

By way of explanation, I'll lead up to what happened like this:

Bonnie's complacency about Jay was driving me insane. Treavor's sisters, and dykes, and innocent, handicapped girls – Bonnie had a justification for every one of Jay's obvious assignations. But I knew that they weren't innocent; I knew he was a cheating son of a bitch. I could tell from the way he looked at me.

But stupid Bonnie explained away all of my evidence, turned her back on the truth. I frequently thought that the only way her eyes would be opened was if she (or I) would actually catch him in the hay with someone. Then even she couldn't deny how he really was.

The events that landed me here occurred last Saturday afternoon. I'm not so far gone with trauma and medication and institutionalization not to know what day it is. Bonnie had something at school, so Jay had gone to work, or at least that's where he said he'd gone. Treavor had gone to visit his sister, the doctor. Something about a back sprain. I dunno; whatever it was, it hadn't affected his performance in bed.

So, I was alone at the big apartment at the foot of the hill. I'd used the rarity of an empty apartment to enjoy a long, hot bubble bath, and was lounging around in my bathrobe. I started to think about Treavor, and that inner monologue led to ruminations about his bed. It was huge and soft, an adult playpen of the most entertaining kind, but it squeaked.

Treavor's bed squeaked so much that sometimes I thought that the whole building could hear us, but it was the idea that *Jay* could hear us (on the infrequent nights that he was home) that annoyed me the most. It was bad enough that I had to curtail my usual expressiveness when I knew he was just on the other side of the wall, but even if I was silent, there was always that rhythmic squeaking. Treavor had a faux brass headboard, and while it was useful in other ways, again, the tradeoff was that squeak. But I figured that the noise could be easily silenced. I'd just go around and tighten all the screws.

Their apartment, I soon discovered, was totally devoid of tools, however. You would've thought that tradesmen would've had a hammer or a drill laying around, but I couldn't even find a screwdriver. Maybe they kept all their tools in their trucks. I would not be stymied, however. I was single-minded in my crusade to kill that tell-tale squeak, so I improvised, MacGyver-stylie. I found a small steak knife in the kitchen, and commenced to tightening the screws with that.

I was working on the last one when I heard the front door open and close. Then there was a thunk, another thunk. I just had time to be happy that Treavor had returned, to look forward to trying out the newly squeakless bed, when Jay walked by the open bedroom door. He was halfway through taking off his shirt; he was barefoot. I realized that the thunking noises had been him taking off his work boots in the living room.

He passed the door, then came back. I was kneeling on the bed, busily working on the last screw with the steak knife. He asked me what I was doing.

I set the knife down on the bedside table and stood up, trying to gracefully conceal my partial nudity with my robe. I hadn't expected *him,* after all, had been trying to be alluring for Treavor. I came around to the other side and sat on the bed, and told him I was fixing the squeaky headboard.

I expected him to grin or wiggle his black eyebrows at me, but Jay the Player was in Serious Salteesiak mode at the minute. He leaned one sculptured arm against the doorframe; his shirt hung open, revealing his smooth, perfect chest. He said, "We need to talk, Susie."

The diminutive annoyed me. Anytime someone called me Susie, I immediately felt as though they were talking down to me, and it was doubly so with people I didn't like, such as Jay. But I could guess what he wanted to talk about – Bonnie is such a blabbermouth – and maybe it was time to clear the air. Or pollute it with invective. Maybe it was time that I at last accused him to his face.

I pulled my robe up tighter around my throat and gestured for him to come in. To sit beside me.

"So talk."

Jay sat, and I was satisfied at my repair job: the bed didn't squeak.

"I'd like to know why you keep telling Bonnie all these stories about me. Why you have it in for me."

"I don't have it in for you, Jay." *You smug, cheating, son of a bitch.*

"Then, why do you keep trying to convince Bonnie . . .? What have I ever done to you, Susie? I told you before – I like you."

Jay put his hand on my cheek and I was instantaneously reminded of Peter, a lifetime ago. And just like Peter, Jay kissed me then, slowly, and before I quite knew what I was doing, I was kissing him back. Just like with my stepbrother, kissing Bonnie's incredible boyfriend sparked electricity I'd only dreamt about, launched the jungle-beat thrumming of the blood in my ears. But I knew what to do with the dark urgency now.

Without any hesitation at all, Jay rolled me backwards onto Treavor's bed. He pushed open my robe and commenced to performing all those acts that I had long ago guessed that he would be so good at. I gripped the bars of the brass headboard in some kind of a disbelieving (though not hardly surprised) orgasmic fugue. Then Jay stood, threw off his shirt, and dropped his pants. Again, I was stunned but not at all surprised.

He sprang onto the bed and fell onto me, and I clung to his neck, cried out, bit him hard on the shoulder, because it was exactly as entirely amazing as I'd always known it would be. Jay was a thoroughbred, *that fast horse.* He was all about the giddy-up, that coarse, no-frills Pony Express gallop through the sage toward oblivion. Just the way I like it.

It seemed to go on for a lifetime, but try as I might, I can remember only snatches: deep, devouring kisses; quick, wordless, anticipation-filled pauses between position changes. The dislike I felt for him manifesting itself into rough, hard, sliding, thrusting bliss.

I finally collapsed acrost his chest, panting, winded. Goddamn, it was inconceivable how good he was! But that didn't mean I liked him. If anything, my hatred had been burnished to a new glow by his ravaging seduction. I reveled in my own arrogance: I had his cheating ass now. Bonnie would see . . .

"I guess you like me, too," Jay said then. He pushed the sweaty hair out of my eyes and gave me his trademark, devastating, crooked grin, then continued. "I always thought you had a thing for me, Susie. The way you stare at me, even in front of Bonnie. I don't think it bothers her, though. She trusts you."

The bastard had the nerve to *wink* at me.

"I've always felt bad that Bonnie met me first, though. That you never got your chance."

"Until now."

Jay's grin widened. "You know, to make it up to you – me being with Bonnie – I thought if I talked Treavor into seeing you – hell, he said he didn't think he'd like a brainy chick – but you've surprised him."

As the gist of what he was saying sunk into my mind, a white hot anger, molten, started to form in front of my eyes. The only reason Treavor had shown an interest in me was because Jay had told him to. I felt like Rosemary must've, when she figured out that her husband was in on it, too. At first, she'd believed that it had to be just the old devil worshippers. But, no. Her nice-guy husband was not only in on it, it had been he who'd sold her out.

Jay wasn't the only devil here. Nice-guy Treavor was his boy, after all, and Jay was still going on about Blondie's impressions of me. "He told me I was right. He said, 'Damn, Sam, the way she looks at you! Like you're on the menu!' He was hesitant to go for it, but I'm here to tell ya that after the first couple of times – he's all down now. He jokes that you're probably thinking about me, but you're doing him, so . . . He's not the jealous type, anyway."

On and on, Jay talked. "I thought you'd stop checking me out once Treavor worked his magic, but it didn't work that way, did it? It only got worse for you, huh? I could tell, when you started in on all these accusations. You still think I'm a thief, and now, I'm cheating on Bonnie. I told her, 'They call that projection, when someone accuses someone of what they want to do themselves.' And damned if I wasn't right. All along, I told Bonnie, 'She wants me, baby, that's why she keeps telling you I'm cheating on you, because she wants it to be her–'"

I swept the steak knife from the bedside table, flipped it over in my hand, and stabbed Jay then. It was bad enough that he and Treavor were in it together; that he had sicced his lover on me to keep me quiet and sated, so I'd stop *wanting him.* But the idea that he'd discussed it all with Bonnie; that the *three* of them had probably sat around and had a good laugh at the ridiculous idea that I could ever *want* Jay Salteesiak . . .

My first blow should've done some serious damage: in my fury, I'd drawn my arm all the way back and brought it down with all the force I had. But my fury also blinded me, and my aim was way off. I almost missed entirely, burying the knife in the mattress and only nicking a fairly good chunk out of Jay's muscled collarbone.

He reacted like a coward, pushing me off of him and trying to flee. But halfway out of the bed, he got tangled in the sheets. He fell, hit his head on the floor. That didn't hurt him, but it stunned him for a second, and I leapt up, then dropped to my knees, and straddled him. I brought the knife down again. He put his arm up, and I sliced him a glancing cut to the meaty part of his forearm. The words went through my head – I might've even said them out loud: "They call that a defensive wound, Lover Boy. Still think I want you now?" I cocked my arm back again.

But then Treavor was in the room, shouting, pulling me off of Jay. He held me by the shoulders and shook me. I dropped the knife. He yelled questions, mostly, 'What the fuck are you doing, Sue?' His face was an array of disbelieving question marks.

I burst into tears, screamed, "He raped me!" But still the angry, questioning look remained on Treavor's face.

He looked down at the rapist, still on the floor, bleeding. I looked down at Jay, too, and it was the funniest thing. His shirt was soaked red on the arm and near the neck – but when did he have time to put *his shirt* – and *his pants!* – back on?

It made no sense at all. I'd just enjoyed the greatest fuck of my life, and then he'd started to run his mouth about how I had wanted it all along, and then I had just snapped. He had to stop talking. I had to shut him up. It was so ridiculous, I'd never wanted him, I just went along with it so I could prove it to Bonnie, and the fact that it had been great just like I knew it was gonna be, didn't have anything to do with that. It was immaterial how much I'd liked it. He was a cheating son of a bitch, but how did he get his clothes back on?

It didn't make any sense! I heard a rushing in my ears and black dots started to bounce in front of my eyes, and then I passed out.

When I woke up, I was in Treavor's bed, and a blonde woman was taking my pulse. "'I'm Dr. Bronkaid," she said. What kind of a name was that? "Can you tell me what happened?"

Oh, hell, no. I wasn't going to miss the family resemblance twice. The sympathetic, soft-spoken lady doctor had to be Treavor's sister Stephanie. Another member of the clan, and no friend of mine. I screamed and burst into hysterical tears again.

"Jay raped me!" I sobbed and tried to get out of the bed. Treavor ran in and held me down; I noticed that he had blood on his shirt. His sister produced a hypo from I know not where.

"This'll calm you down, honey."

I just had time to think *chemical restraint* before I was out.

I came to the following morning and discovered that I was now an inmate in the Laughing College. When I asked how I got here, the nurse said Dr. Bronkaid had admitted me. In her professional opinion, I was hysterical and might be a danger to myself or others. The nurse smiled kindly and confided that *she* thought that I was just confused and needed rest. *I'm not sick, but I'm not well . . .*

The nurse told me to report to group therapy at nine o'clock, to talk about my problems with everyone else. Like I say, I haven't had much to say. I told them I'm not ready to discuss it yet.

I guess this is what I get for stabbing my stepsister's boyfriend. I guess I should be glad I'm not in jail. But when Dr. Crowell asks me why I did it, I'm sticking to the rape story.

When Bonnie visited, I told *her* that Jay raped me – flat out, softly, a tear running down my cheek. She said coldly, "That isn't possible, Susan, and after you talk to the doctors, I'm sure they'll help you to see that."

Then she would say no more about it.

I wondered idly why Treavor hadn't come to see me, but then on the other hand, Jay had probably told him what we had done. I could picture him saying, "It wasn't hardly rape, my pet."

And though Treavor wasn't *the jealous type,* he was a man, after all, and just like any other man, he would side with his buddy. I was sure that, in some kind of twisted male logic, it was okay for his best friend and lifetime pal, his *lover,* to betray him with me, but it wasn't okay for me to betray *him,* with anybody. I was the bad guy, and Jay was, as always, golden.

Plus, there was the fact that I had just snapped at the whole sick situation and stabbed Treavor's *brother.* But it was all okay. Treavor and I were through, regardless. We were through the second that Jay told me that Blondie had only agreed to see me because he'd suggested it.

Crazy, Over the Rainbow, I am Crazy, Bars in the Window...

My showdown with the good doctor finally arrived, and I record what was said here because I am positively nonplussed.

It started professionally enough. Dr. Crowell asked me what had happened last Saturday, and I told him succinctly, "Jay Salteesiak raped me."

"Are you sure, Susan? Are you sure you didn't just . . . I won't ask, are you sure you're not just making it up? Because you don't seem the type to do something like that. Such an accusation is very serious. I think that you're genuinely distraught, sincerely concerned that your sister's boyfriend is deceiving her. So I don't think you're consciously lying about what occurred. But I will ask, are you sure you didn't just . . . dream it?"

It was a kind of a dream, I guess. I had surely dreamt of it before – not as a rape, because it certainly wasn't that – but it sounded better that way. Bonnie, poor, lovesick Bonnie, might've forgiven Jay, otherwise. If I said it was just one of those things that happen sometimes between men and women when they find themselves alone – like Treavor, she never would've forgiven me, but there was a good chance that Jay would've gotten a pass. I would've been the villain, for not refusing. But if it was rape . . . why, hee, hee, it wasn't like I *could* refuse, could I?

"I bit him," I told the doctor simply. That it was out of passion, and not out of some kind of self-defense – he didn't have to know that. "There has to be some kind of report . . .

Treavor's sister knocked me out, but didn't you people examine me?"

"Of course. Whenever there are allegations of this nature . . .""

Dr. Crowell produced a piece of paper from my file and pushed it across the desk at me. I scanned it. The bottom line: no evidence of sexual assault. No evidence of sexual contact of any kind. No bruises, no abrasions, external or internal, no fluids not my own. The only DNA – *Mr. Salteesiak states that subject scratched him, and blood under her fingernails –*

"Scratched him?"

The doctor seized on this nonsensical detail. "Does that surprise you? You don't remember scratching him?"

Again the picture of Jay laying on the floor, stunned, bleeding – but fully clothed – tried to impress itself on my mind. If anything was a dream, it was *that*. It hadn't hardly been rape, but I knew what we'd done together. Why did I keep seeing him dressed?

Are you sure you're not just making it up?

Was I?

A warning voice in my head asked, *Just what the fuck is going on here?*

"No. I don't remember scratching him. What does he say happened?"

"I only have Dr. Bronkaid's report. She states that she and Mr. Carruthers heard you and Mr. Salteesiak having some kind of altercation. Her brother went down the hall to investigate. You started screaming that Mr. Salteesiak had raped you; it was obvious to the doctor that he had not. You fainted, then when you woke up, you started screaming again, so she sedated you." He glanced at the file. "Sometime during the altercation, you scratched Mr. Salteesiak; that's why there was blood under your fingernails when you were admitted, obviously his blood. But there was no evidence of–"

"I read it." I slid the paper back at him. "And there were no other marks on him, besides this . . . *scratch?"*

The doctor shook his head firmly. "Not according to Dr. Bronkaid's statement. I talked to her when they brought you in, Susan. She said that, based on what you claimed, she examined Mr. Salteesiak thoroughly. There were no bite marks on him."

"Nothing but this scratch."

Dr. Crowell nodded, looked at me expectantly, waiting for me to say something. But I was dumbstruck, because I realized that I was in the middle of a cover-up.

Dr. Bronkaid had judged me to be hysterical, a danger to myself and others; she'd shot me up with a sedative – did doctors just carry around sedatives? What kind of a doctor was she, anyway? Then she'd called the men in the white coats, had me committed, consulted with the PhD that was assigned to me.

But somehow, in all that excitement, the fact that I'd stabbed Jay at least twice had been overlooked. Dr. Bronkaid, Treavor, and even Jay himself were all covering for me. They'd wiped away the majority of Jay's blood, mostly *washed this filthy witness from my hand.* They'd cleaned up whatever mess remained, disposed of the weapon. I guess I should've felt grateful for all that. No wonder there hadn't been any cops in to interview me.

But wait a minute. Hold on just a goddamn second, here. If it wasn't my homicidal rage that had landed me in the nuthouse . . . Screaming rape didn't get you *chemically restrained* and locked up. I imagined it got you a couple of Valiums, maybe, and a visit to a regular hospital, with gentle, compassionate nurses. No matter how hysterical you were about it. It didn't get you an injected Mickey Finn; it didn't land you in the asylum under a suicide watch.

"Why exactly am I here, Dr. Crowell?"

He sighed. "You're claiming a rape that never happened, Susan. Mr. Carruthers and his sister – they were in the other room. Mr. Salteesiak came in to talk to you, then he says you started screaming at him."

"He claims there was no–" *Incredible sex?*

"No assault. And the evidence confirms it. I'm here to help you figure out why you think there was."

Again, he waited for me to speak. But I had nothing. I remembered it so clearly, though in snatches: Jay's body, his kisses; everything I'd ever thought about him and how it would be . . . But Dr. Crowell, and more importantly, the *evidence,* said it hadn't been.

My first thought was that the whitewash stretched farther than just Jay and Treavor and the unfortunately named Dr. Bronkaid. They'd covered up the stabbing – thanks, guys – but they were also covering up the sex.

While it was true that I'd been under a lot of stress lately – Bonnie's utter refusal to see her boyfriend for what he really was, the way he always stared at me like he wanted to eat me – yeah, all that had been weighing on my mind, occupying the majority of my thoughts. Stress could do a number on a person – hadn't it driven Bonnie to try to kill herself?

But all the stress in the world wasn't going to drive me to see conspiracies where none could possibly exist. My, for lack of a better word, my *friends* – had covered up an attempted murder, but there was no way they could've covered up the aftermath of the callisthenic sex in which Jay and I had engaged. And there was no reason that Dr. Crowell and *The Center for Flaccid Minds* would want to cover it up, either. Doctors are chummy, but not that chummy. It wasn't like Jay was a public figure or something.

I'd hysterically claimed to've been raped, and when I was brought in, they'd dutifully examined me. But the no-doubt thorough health care professionals had found no evidence of rape. They'd found no evidence of any sexual contact *at all.*

I went over it again in my head. I'd been half-dressed, still feeling all warm and squishy from my nice bath. Then irresistible Jay had been sitting there beside me on the bed, telling me he liked me . . .

Christ, had I really dreamed the whole thing? Had I stabbed Jay for telling me that he'd always known I'd wanted him? Did I stab him because he told me that Treavor only wanted me because he'd told him to? Christ, had I even stabbed him at all?

No. It just wasn't possible. I knew what I remembered.

Suddenly, I really did feel confused. I really did think I needed a rest. The doctor was waiting for me to speak. "I gotta think about this," I told him, just so he'd let me out of his office, so I could go back to my room. Write it all down. Try to figure it out.

"Of course, Susan. Have you had all your medication for today?"

"Just the morning one."

"I'll have the nurse give you your second dose before dinner. We'll talk again, whenever you're ready."

BONNIE'S JOURNAL, PART ELEVEN

It was already over when I got back from class.

Jay was sitting on the couch, shirtless, smoking a cigarette. I had time to marvel that Jay didn't smoke. There was another guy there, and he was picking bloody gauze off of the coffee table and putting skinny metal instruments and other medical stuff into a black leather satchel-thing. Treavor introduced him – his name was Fred or Ted or Ed or something. Treavor said that he was a friend of Stephanie's, an intern or a resident or some other doctor word. I don't know. I noticed the spidery black stitches on Jay's collarbone and everything else was blotted from my mind.

Fred said something to him about coming in to have the stitches removed in a few days, said he was glad to meet me, then picked up his bag. Treavor saw him to the door. I knelt on the floor in front of Jay, the tears already running down my face.

"What happened?" I cried. It had to've been some kind of accident at work . . .

"Sue stabbed him." Treavor sighed and plopped down on the couch.

I looked at Jay, thinking of course that Treavor was joking, and that it wasn't at all funny. He held up his arm and I saw the wicked slash there, drawn together with more black sutures.

Jay explained that Sue had been fixing Treavor's headboard – Jesus, did it squeak! – with a steak knife, of all incomprehensible things.

On the coffee table, there was a short tumbler of something brown, and he dropped his cigarette into it. I heard it sizzle. Beside the glass, there was a stray piece of reddened gauze that Ed had missed. I shuddered and thought that if anyone needed a drink right then, it was *me*.

Jay continued. "I went in there and asked her why she keeps accusing me of cheating on you. I asked her . . ." Now Jay grinned sheepishly, in embarrassment. "I asked her if it was because she wanted me for herself. I asked her if Treavor wasn't good enough for her anymore." He glanced at his friend and Treavor rolled his eyes. "I'm sorry, Bonnie. I guess it was a fucked up thing to say, but she's kinda been pissing me off with all these constant accusations. So I asked her if it was some kind of projection, that she kept telling you I was cheating on her because she wanted me to cheat on you with her." Again the sheepish smile. "She didn't like what I was saying, I guess, so she stabbed me."

Treavor took up the story. "Steph and I were out here. The three of us had all come up the steps at the same time, and Jay went back to change. We heard him talking to Sue, then we heard her screaming, so I ran in there to see what was going on. She was sitting on him, on the floor, about to stab him again, so I pulled her off him. She was screaming . . ." Treavor stopped.

Jay touched my arm so I'd look at him, and now the embarrassed smile was gone. He was one hundred percent serious. "She was screaming that I'd raped her, Bonnie."

Just when I thought I couldn't be more shocked and amazed at what they were telling me. I was speechless, couldn't even say, *"What?"*

Treavor said, "After screaming that Jay had raped her, Sue passed out and Steph and I put her in the bed. Steph looked at Jay's cuts, then went out and got her bag out of the car. She found that she didn't have any sutures, so she called Teddy to come over and stitch him up." He looked at Jay, grinned faintly. "I thought he was never gonna leave."

"Hell, Treav. It was dinner and a show for him." Jay grinned also.

Treavor went on with the incredible story. "So, Jay's out here in the living room with me. Teddy's laying out all his equipment, getting ready to stitch him up. Steph's in there with Sue. Does she do drugs, Bonnie? Something we don't know about?"

I shook my head, still unable to form words.

"She woke up and started screaming that Jay raped her again. I ran in there – she was hysterical, Bonnie, completely. I held her down and Steph gave her a sedative. Steph thought Sue might hurt herself, or try to hurt Jay again, so she called for an ambulance, and then went with her to the hospital."

"The hospital? *Had* she hurt herself?" God, what next?

"Not that kind of hospital," Treavor said darkly. "Steph said Sue was having some kind of a breakdown. She was delusional, screaming about rapes that hadn't happened. It was dangerous, so Steph had her admitted to the . . . mental hospital."

The next morning, I broke the news to Vanessa and Dad. I told them about the rape thing, that Steph had hospitalized Susan. I didn't tell them about the stabbing part, because Jay had asked me not to. He felt sorry for Sue, said she was sick. No need to burden her mom with all the sad details.

Vanessa was as speechless as I'd been – her eyes got all big and round and she immediately left the room. Dad couldn't contain his mirth, made his crude comment about Susan wanting to take my man. The two of them were no help at all to me.

I called and asked to talk to Sue's doctor. He said that my concern was understandable, and I could rest assured that my sister was receiving the best care possible.

I gave it another day, then went out to the hospital to visit. Susan seemed surprised to see me, and she had that uncharacteristic attitude of rudeness about her, snatching her notebook away and telling me that what it contained was none of my business. Then she started to cry and told me that Jay had raped her.

My lack of pity surprised me. Her tears were meaningless. What she was saying – it was just ridiculous.

Steph warned me not to mention to Sue's doctor that she'd assaulted Jay, either. I thought it was damn nice of Steph to go along with his wishes that way. The fact that Susan had stabbed him was an embarrassment to Jay, and since he's like family to her, Steph agreed to leave it off the report when she admitted Sue to the hospital. One helps cover up one's family embarrassments, I guess, even if one is a medical professional.

"And they'll never let Sue out if the doctor hears that there was violence," Treavor added with a totally not-apropos giggle. He pronounced it *vi-O-lence* and grinned at Jay.

After I visited Susan, I talked to her doctor again. He just kept looking down at her file the whole time, but he did explain the reason for Sue's crazy allegations of rape. He said that sometimes people got caught up in things that were happening inside their heads, things that they only imagined. Things that aren't real at all. Then they reacted to those false things in the real world. He didn't use the word *snapped,* but that's what he was saying.

I'd told him that Sue had repeatedly accused Jay of cheating on me, so he concluded his explanation by saying, "What better way to prove it to you than to say he raped her?"

If that's not crazy, I don't know what is.

The doctor assured me again. He said that with some counseling and some medication, Susan would be better in no time. She would see that this mythical rape had never happened.

But I couldn't help but wonder if what Jay had *NOT* said was the real truth. When he'd jokingly asked Susan if she wanted him for herself, had Sue made a pass at him then? Had she said something like, "You know, Jay, you're right. Why don't we just . . . It'll be our secret"?

And when he turned her down – was that why she'd flipped out and attacked him?

I remembered what she'd told me about Oscar's Radar: "It means that in any situation, the simplest solution is usually the correct one." In this situation – sure, Sue might've been insulted that Jay had accused her of having a thing for him. It was a mean thing for him to ask – isn't Treavor good enough? But her reaction to a playful joke was off the charts. You don't stab somebody over a little insult.

Not unless it was true. Sue had always given me the impression that she didn't like Jay, and I'd always thought that was crazy in and of itself – how could anyone not like Jay? He's great. But then I'd catch her looking at him sometimes, and yeah, it seemed like she might be thinking about things you shouldn't be thinking about your sister's boyfriend, but he's adorable, so I thought it was only natural. So, at the time, her stares made me proud more than jealous.

Jealousy – we covered a play about it in class, just the other day. Thank you, Google – here's what Shakespeare said: Iago hated Othello so much that he planned to *put the Moor at least into a jealousy so strong that judgment cannot cure.* He would practice *upon his peace and quiet even to madness.*

Is that how it's been all this time? Susan, seeing how happy Jay and I are together, while she wanted him all along – did her jealousy about that drive her nuts?

Pity for her isn't coming. I'm finding it very hard to continue to love her right now. She has Treavor. Jay's mine. I'm sorry she's where she is, but she should've had more control over herself.

This Is the Strangest Life I've Ever Known

I walked slowly back down the hall to my room, pondering the things that Dr. Crowell had pointed out to me. *No evidence of sexual assault.* No bite marks on Jay. I'd scratched him, that's why I had his blood under my fingernails when I was admitted.

Jesus, was I really cracking up? Had I really hallucinated the whole thing?

If all these revelations weren't enough for my obviously teetering mind, like the guy from *'Twas the Night Before Christmas,* what to my wondering eyes should appear when I walked into my room, but Peter Cox. Like something from a cartoon, I blinked, rubbed my eyes. Maybe I was imagining him, too.

He was sitting on my bed, looking good enough to eat, as always. He was not, thank Christ, reading my composition book, tucked as it was beneath my pillow, under the hospital corners of the neatly made bed.

I wanted to rush into his arms, to hug him – I saw the same reflex in his eyes. But a lifetime of societal correctness stayed us. The look we exchanged communicated all.

He was supposed to be my brother, after all, and that was the only reason they'd let him wait for me here in my room. Male relatives were permitted visiting time in one's booby hatch cell, but the hospital had a rather provincial rule about visiting boyfriends or husbands. I knew that if he'd ever bothered to come and see her, Angela would've had to reunite with her husband in the day room. Our keepers didn't want any hanky-panky (or violence of the domestic kind, for that matter) occurring between spouses on their watch.

Despite the fact that I could tell that he wanted to give me a hug, Peter didn't smile at me, however. "What the fuck, Sue? What the hell happened?"

When I heard his voice, his tone, chock full of annoyed concern, I knew he was really there. But to tell the God's honest truth, before he spoke, I wasn't completely sure.

I decided to run the ol' hallucination up the flag pole, just to see if he'd salute it. "Bonnie's boyfriend raped me."

His response was instantaneous: "That's not what she says. Or him."

I thought that I just might incur a genuine nervous breakdown if I was subjected to one more impossibility today. *"You talked to Bonnie?"*

"Yes, Sue. I talked to Bonnie. You're in the nuthouse, for God's sake. She called me, and I went over there. I talked to them–"

"Jay, too?"

"Yeah. And Lucius Malfoy." When I didn't immediately ken that he was referring to Treavor's blondeness, Peter added, "Yeah, he didn't get it either." He shook his head. "Christ, Sue. He's as dumb as a bag of wet hammers. I don't see how you can stand him. I don't care how big his–"

"What did they tell you?" I didn't want to talk about Treavor. He was ancient history. I never wanted to see him again. He was Jay's *pet;* he did his bidding on command. They could have each other.

Peter considered me for a long second. "That you got in some kind of argument with Jack–"

"Jay."

"Whatever. You got into some kind of argument with Bonnie's man, then flipped out and stabbed him."

So the stabbing part *did* happen. I didn't know if that reassured me or made me more worried.

"Sir Tristan the Blonde said he pulled you off of the victim, and you started screaming about how he'd raped you, so they 5150'd you." Peter gave me a curious look, accompanied by the ghost of a grin. "How was that ambulance ride? Did they put you in a straitjacket?"

"I don't remember it. Treavor's sister shot me up with something."

The ginger eyebrows went up in that inimitable, quizzical Peter way, and I realized how much I'd missed him.

Peter's smile fled. "She *shot you up?* Jesus, Sue! What kind of people are you hanging around with?"

"She's a doctor, Pete, for Christ's sake. She's the one that had me committed."

"Had me committed. Just the thing you want to post on your Facebook page. Jesus, Sue," he repeated and shook his head again.

His disapprobation stung me a little bit, but then, sympathy had never been Peter's long suit, especially not when disaster struck people who had only done it to themselves. Politicians caught with their hands in the kitty, or picked up in prostitution stings; or even overly-romantic stepsisters that loved not wisely but too well. *"The wages of sin is death,"* Peter would say, and shrug at the stupidity of it all. This complete lack of maudlin sentimentality was one of the things I'd always liked about him.

But maybe I thought I deserved some of his pity right at the moment. I was confused. I was in the goddamned asylum, for crying out loud.

"What happened?" he repeated, more annoyed now.

I could show annoyance, too. I could be stubborn. "Jay raped me. So I stabbed him." *Fuck you, Pete Cox, and anyone that even looks like you.*

"I met him, Sue. He's just as dumb as Travis—"

"Treavor."

"Whatever. It's obvious why Bonnie's all in love with him. He's never had to rape anybody." Peter's eyes were just as jade green and angry as a carved statue of a Chinese fu dog. Then he smiled, and the anger was gone. "It's me you're talking to, Sue. I know you."

139

From a mile away, I saw the scope and sight on the rifle of his impending character assassination, so I asked, with a full measure of affront, "What do you know?"

"You've been saying all along that this guy's a bastard. A thief. That he cheats on Bonnie. I saw what he looks like, so, I figure, you thought you might just go ahead and find out how shady he was willing to be."

I was appalled. "Is this supposed to be some kind of tough love kinda thing? You come in here, all pissed off, then insult me? You think I'm gonna freak out, try to stab you, too?"

He laughed. "I *would* like to see you in a straitjacket."

"Christ, Peter! I'd never betray Bonnie like that!"

"Wouldn't you?" Peter blinked slowly at me, his smile like the Cheshire Cat. "Wouldn't I? What did Bonnie ever mean to us?"

I opened and closed my mouth like a beached fish, the defense springing immediately to my mind, a defense that wouldn't stand up in Morality Court: What he and I did – that wasn't the same thing as nailing her two-timing boyfriend. It was *our thing,* our secret–

"Did he turn you down? Is that why you stabbed him?"

No. That couldn't possibly be it.

Could it?

Peter hopped off the bed and began pacing the room. "I don't really care what happened, Sue, but everybody knows Jack didn't rape you. I know it, he knows it. Bonnie and your brain trust of a pretty boyfriend know it. And the cops–"

"There were no cops."

Again his eyebrows went up.

"I told you. Treavor's sister is a doctor. She sedated me and had me brought here, but apparently they didn't tell anybody that I stabbed Jay. The intake report only said that I scratched him. So, no cops."

"And you're dumb enough to be running your mouth off about a rape that didn't happen?"

"That's why I'm here, Pete, don't you get it? Because the rape didn't happen. Apparently, nothing happened, but because

I told them it did – because I thought it did – that's why I'm here."

"What the fuck, Sue?" Peter shook his head again, firmly. "I don't care. All I know is, I've gotta get you out of here."

That was a flash of humanity from him. I liked that, but then a darker thought struck me. "Look, Pete. The truth is – like I say, I thought something did happen. It wasn't rape, but . . . I'm a little confused right now."

He was surprised at that, but then shook his head again. "It doesn't matter. You're gonna have to tell 'em whatever they want to hear. Or they'll keep you in here forever."

"Maybe I should stay here for a while . . ." At his shocked expression, I added quickly, "I dunno. I thought it happened . . . just like you said. That Jay started to kiss me, then we . . . I swear to God, Pete, I remember it so clearly!"

"But it didn't happen."

"No! The report says *no evidence of sexual contact!*" I lowered my voice. "I imagined the whole thing. Christ!" I put my hands over my face. Peter drew them away gently.

"You didn't imagine stabbing him. Even if that's not why they committed you, that *did* happen. Why did you–"

"He started talking about how he and Treavor and *fucking* Bonnie, for Christ's sake – how they'd known all along that I'd wanted him, and here I'd gone ahead and proved it. I swear, I *heard him say that, Pete!* It seemed like . . . I thought I was on top of him, then, that we were . . . that we'd just finished . . ." I shook *my* head now. "And then he wouldn't shut up about it, how he'd told Treavor to sleep with me so I'd stop staring at him. I felt this overwhelming urge then, Pete. This hot bolt of hatred. I had to shut him up. So I grabbed the knife and I stabbed him."

Peter continued to pace the room. "None of it matters now. Whatever he said – you know you didn't fuck him, that he surely didn't rape you. You know it didn't happen. You've come to your senses."

Did I? Had I? It still seemed so real.

141

"You're all right now. I've gotta get you out of here." Peter paced; he cogitated. Then he snapped his fingers. "They put Bonnie on antidepressants, right? After she tried to kill herself?"

I nodded. "Paxil. They're giving me some kind of–"

"What? What are they giving you?" The eyebrows again.

"I'm not really sure. Something to make me calmer–"

"Jesus, God, Sue! What did I tell you about that stuff? It fucks with your brain chemistry!" He viciously tapped the side of his head. "People get sad, they get bored, and instead of telling them to man up and get over it, these doctors feed them that shit, and before you know it, they need it! If they don't get their fix, they feel like zombies! How could you let them make you take–"

"I didn't have a whole lot of choice."

"Haven't you ever seen – in the movies – where people pretend to take their pills, then spit them out?"

I could've said, *I thought it would help,* but that would've just caused Peter to go on another anti-antidepressant tirade, like he was Tom Cruise or something. So I didn't say anything.

"Forget about what they're giving you now. But don't, I beseech you, take any more of it. I love you, Sue. I don't want them messing up your brain."

Wait, what? Did Peter just say he loved me? Or that he just loved my brain?

"Bonnie still has some Paxil?" he asked.

"What?" It was like I was in some kind of slow motion all of a sudden, like I was one sentence behind. *I love you, Sue.*

"I said, do you think Bonnie still has some Paxil?"

"Yeah. She stopped taking them when she met Mr. Wonderful. The bottle's probably still in her medicine chest."

Peter grinned then, that delightful, devious ol'Peter smile. He said to his phone, "Paxil horror stories."

He scrolled, then said, "Okay. Here's what you tell 'em. You were feeling sad, because Bonnie was all happy and in love, and you weren't." Again he grinned at me – how

142

ridiculous was that? Had I ever dreamed of happily ever afters, like Bonnie did? Peter didn't think so.

He continued. "You tell the doctor that since Bonnie wasn't taking her Paxil, you decided to self-medicate yourself out of your sadness. But people shouldn't take that shit if they're not under the care of a physician, and damned if it didn't make you go all loopy. You hallucinated. You really believed that Jack was gonna–"

"Jay."

"Whatever. You really believed that he was *gonna* rape you. And since you've been in here, taking whatever else they've been giving you . . . Hell, tell 'em that it's worked. You know he didn't. You remember that it was all just a dream, and you're sorry, but you're better now."

"But–"

"No buts, Susie. I gotta get you outta here. You tell 'em whatever it takes."

Peter hugged me then, and hey, yeah, it's all right for a stepbrother and stepsister to hug, especially when the stepsister was locked up in a mental hospital. When she was confused; *loopy.* But there was an odd quality to his hug, something I'd never felt from him before. I don't know how to describe it, but I'll try. Peter *squeezed* me; he clung to me; it was like the lyrics to that song, like I was sixteen again, and had just been rickrolled: *Never gonna give you up, never gonna let you down* . . .

Peter stopped hugging me, but I could feel his reluctance to let me go. It was so strange. He didn't let me go entirely, but held me at arm's length. He squeezed my hands, held them for another long second.

"Is this pity?" I asked.

He snorted laughter. "You would think that."

"What's with you?"

I felt like I was in *The Twilight Zone* again, in the psych ward section of it. My gloriously intelligent stepbrother and me, no slouch at a clever turn of phrase myself, had been reduced to three and four word, fairly meaningless sentences. Another one came to mind: *What the fuck?*

"I've been thinking, Sue."

Four words, this time.

"A dangerous pastime, on the best of days."

Peter ignored my attempt at humor, remained serious. "It had crossed my mind, even before . . . *this.*" He gestured at my quarters, dropped his hands. "You know, Sarah moved out."

"Who?"

A faint chuckle. "I guess I deserve that."

I concentrated. I'd been completely serious. Who was Sarah? Oh, yeah. Sarah was his roommate-girlfriend. I'd never met her, never even seen a picture of her. I'd never really cared too much about her existence. Peter's relationships never lasted, any more than mine did, so why should I bother remembering her name?

My brain felt clouded, I mean, like literally, like there were clouds forming inside my head, like one of those time-lapse films of an oncoming rain storm. Maybe it was the medication – maybe Pete shouldn't be hating on it so much. It was a nice feeling, like there was a knock on the door and I knew that when I answered it, it was going to be something good. I couldn't imagine what it might be, but hey, maybe this was how one felt when one's serotonin uptake was selectively inhibited. Calm. Happy about the future. There was an anticipation of some great thing, like you feel when you're a kid and it's Christmas Eve.

Or maybe it had something to do with Peter's odd behavior. Lingering hugs. Holding my hands. It was like old times, like whenever we'd been alone. I'd always shared a wonderful kind of affection with my stepbrother, born of complete trust. We *knew* each other. It was something I'd never achieved with anybody else.

But this was weird, his seeming inability to get his point across, the pauses, the self-deprecating chuckles. Peter was a lot of things, but self-deprecating had never been one of them. Again I asked him, "What's with you?"

144

"Like I say, Ive been thinking. Maybe you and me . . . Maybe you should come and live with me at the beach."

Now I snorted laughter, because my very first thought was, "Yeah. It's not like I probably have a job to go back to."

Again, an awkward pause, again that feeling that I was a sentence behind in the conversation. Wasn't it his turn to say something now?

He looked at the floor, actually scuffed at the carpet with the toe of his shoe, like he was, I dunno, *shy?* Reluctant to spit out whatever it was he was trying to communicate? I thought, *Who are you, and what have you done with Peter?*

Then I reversed my earlier opinions on the medication – it wasn't Peter, it was me. He was the same as he'd always been: my sardonic, cynical other half. Peter wasn't suddenly become at a loss for words. It was just my altered perception. It was the drugs.

He looked up, grabbed my hand so suddenly that it made me jump. "What I'm trying to say is this, Sue. We're not kids anymore. We don't need to pretend to be . . . I want you to come to the beach with me. No one there even knows I have a stepsister. I want us to be . . . together."

Pictures of my Georges and Dannys and Brandons bloomed in my mind; they smiled, waved. And then there appeared all of Peter's Cindys and Debbies, Marias and *Bonnies.* They also waved, all innocent and unknowing about what was going on between Peter and me, right under their noses, all behind their wouldn't-have-suspected-it-for-a-minute backs.

"Just like the old days," I said, but then another thought impressed itself through the warm, sweet cotton candy that had become my mind. "How could we pull it off now? Didn't you say your place is only a one bedroom?"

"Not like the old days, Sue. What I'm saying – I want us to be together, just the two of us. Nobody else. No more pretending we're something we're not. Something we never were. I've been thinking about this for a long time."

When I just looked at him, dumbfounded, he babbled on. "Nobody has to know that we grew up together. How would they know? It's not like we have the same last name. We wouldn't have to tell Vanessa – we would just say we were roommates, we wouldn't like, rub her nose in it – and John . . . he wouldn't care. John can fuck right off, regardless. It's not like he's gonna be bringing your mom down for visits, now is he? Especially after . . . this." Peter released my hand and again gestured at our surroundings.

I said, "Are you sure this isn't pity? You just sweep in here – is your white horse double-parked outside? It's always been, *Keep looking, Sue,* and now you want to . . . you want *us* . . ." *To be together?*

I had dreamed of Bonnie's stunning, cheating son of a bitch of a boyfriend enough times. Asleep, waking. Apparently, my mind had just made up *its* mind one day to make it real for me. If only he'd kept his fat mouth shut, maybe I would've realized that it was just a dream, a fugue, some kind of inter-dimensional mental hiccup – maybe I wouldn't have stabbed Jay at all, if he would've *just shut up.*

But this . . . Peter and me, together, *just the two of us* – I'd never even dared to dream of that.

"I'm done looking," he was saying. "You want me to be all soppy, expose my vulnerability? Is that what you want?"

"Will it hurt?"

Peter smiled then, grasped my hand again. "No, it won't hurt. Here it is – I'm done looking. I realized that all I've ever been looking for is you. What d'ya say?"

It wasn't *I love you,* but it it was definitely, *I want you, and only you.* It was most assuredly *I need you.* And that was a lot, coming from Peter. He'd never needed anybody.

Except me, I realized with a kind of awe.

From the depths of memory came Princess Katherine's words from the movie version of *Henry V,* one of Peter's very favorites. I even affected the French accent. *"I cannot tell vhat is dat."*

Peter smiled, dared another non-brotherly hug, supplied the king's line. *"Can any of your neighbors tell, Kate? I'll ask them. Come, I know thou lovest me."*

"I'm serious, Pete. After all the shit that's happened to me in the last week – I don't know anymore. Is this real?"

"You're the only one of them that wasn't crazy, Sue. And you're still not. What's an occasional hallucination on the long road of life? This is real. Tell these assholes whatever they want to hear, so I can get you out of here. *Yassuh, Massuh, it was all a big mistake, I was just confused. I dreamed it all up. Why sure, I'll fill all these prescriptions.*

"Then go home and pack your kit, and come to the beach with me. We belong together. We always have."

It still wasn't *I love you,* but it was good enough.

"All right, Pete. You're on."

"How long do you think it'll take? To convince them that you're . . ."

"The technical term is *better."*

"I'll . . .I'll wait for you," he stammered. How adorable a little taste of uncertainty was on Peter! "I'll get a hotel."

"You don't have to do that. It'll probably take a little while. I'll have to be *evaluated.* Go on home. I'll call you."

But actually, I don't think it'll take long at all, because it'll be true. I'm definitely better now.

BONNIE'S JOURNAL, PART TWELVE

So I guess Susan's supposed to be cured now.

Vanessa called, said she'd just showed up back home. Unannounced, no warning at all. She'd had to ring the doorbell, because she had no keys. I've got her keys and her purse and her phone, because all that was at Jay's when they took her away. Her car's still at Jay's too, sitting on the street, covered in a fine layer of my-owner's-in-the-nuthouse dust.

Vanessa told me that Susan has requested that I bring Jay and Treavor over with me as soon as possible. Sue has big announcements, she says, explanations for the whole family.

Jay doesn't really want to go, and Treavor . . . I actually feel sorrier for him than I feel for Jay. It'll be uncomfortable for Jay, of course, having to listen to whatever my sister has to say, the person that stabbed him, the person that accused him of a rape that didn't happen. All of that's going to be awkward for him, and me as well. But we get to leave, to get away from her once her story's told.

But poor Treavor! He feels sorry for Sue. He's vowed that he'll stick by her, and that he'll try his best to help her work through whatever it was that made her freak out, whatever mental breakdown it was that made her try to kill his best friend – and when that failed, to try to accuse him of a terrible crime. It's obviously a difficult decision for Treavor – to side with his best friend, someone he's known all his life, or to help his girlfriend-of-a-few-months through this difficult time? But he figures that Susan needs him now – who else does she have? He believes it's his duty to stand by her and help her any way he can.

But Jay's confided in me that Treavor is actually miserable about the whole thing. What Susan did – he says he can't really forgive her, even if Jay has; even if I have. Even if it was the result of some mental illness, all cured and gone away now – Treavor really wants out. According to Jay, he keeps saying, "Grandpa always said, 'Never sleep with anyone crazier than you.'" And he doesn't even smile.

I guess his short relationship with Susan has been fun and all to Treavor, but an attempt on Jay's life and a hysterical accusation of sexual assault – these are, quite simply, deal breakers for him. He really wants nothing more to do with my sister. But he feels like he'll damage her fragile mind even further if he abandons her now. He feels like she's his responsibility now, for as long as it takes.

"Until she's well enough that he can dump her without feeling guilty," Jay told me. "He's worried that it might take a long time." With his finger, he made a circle in the air beside his temple, and I giggled despite the fact that it wasn't very nice at all.

I feel sorry for Treavor. He's trapped, and then, when he feels as though he can safely escape from Sue's smothering clutches, then he's gonna be all alone again. While this brush with insanity has left Jay with some stitches, and he'll probably have a couple of scars, he still has me. Treavor's gonna have to endure further trials, and then still wind up with nothing. He's gonna have find a new girl, start all over again.

When I expressed my sorrow about all this, Jay replied with half a grin, "Ah, he'll live. Let's go."

LATER

When we arrived at the house, Sue sat us down at the dining room table. She stood at the head, and I sat at the foot. Jay and Treavor were on one side, Treavor closest to her. Dad and Vanessa sat across from them. I noticed that she would not even look at Treavor. She didn't have any trouble making eye contact with the rest of us; I thought she even smirked rather boldly at Jay, but she wouldn't even glance fondly at this great guy who was willing to stick by her.

"I'd like to beg your forgiveness for the bullshit I've put you all through the last week," she began.

It's been more than a week, I thought. I'd had to listen to all her accusations for way longer than that, about Jay being a thief and that he was cheating on me . . .

"And I'd like to promise you that nothing like it will ever happen again."

It struck me that there was not one single bit of remorse in Susan's tone. It was like she was doing some kind of read-through rehearsal of an apology someone else had written about something someone else had done. She wasn't really begging, and she wasn't really promising. Her voice was light, her words hurried and excited. I wondered what kind of medication she was on. The talk-quickly-be-happy kind, apparently.

"The reason that I'm able to make you this promise is because I'm leaving, moving out, skipping town." Still, Susan wouldn't look at Treavor. If she had, she wouldn't have been able to miss the dawning of stunned relief on his face. Jay frowned at him, and Treavor quickly tried to mask the expression. Susan was definitely not breaking his heart.

"I'm removing myself from all of your lives. I figure, it's the very least I can do. I'm gonna be someone else's problem now." Susan winked at her mom.

Vanessa was not amused. "Whose?" she asked tremulously. She seemed to have aged a decade in the last week. *Your only child being locked up in the home'll do that to you,* I thought.

Susan's grin was as wide as all outdoors. "Peter's."

"What?" I said, before I could stop it from escaping.

"Yeah. Peter's decided that he wants to look after me until I'm fully cured." Susan giggled.

It was all a big joke to her, this idea of being *cured.* She had sliced and diced Jay and accused him of raping her, two very serious things that didn't reflect well on her mental stability. But now she was cured, or on her way, so we were all supposed to be feeling as light-hearted about it as she was. Not only were we supposed to forgive, we were supposed to forget, because of her giggly, not-much of an apology.

It struck me that she wasn't *cured* in the least. Whatever had caused her to snap, this lashing out, this reacting in the real world to what she'd only imagined about Jay in her head – and why did she think it was okay to be imagining anything about Jay in her head, anyway? – I didn't see how that could be just wiped out from Sue's mind after a few days in the booby hatch and a few words from some doctor. Her attitude was like she'd gotten away with something, as if maybe her delusions about Jay hadn't changed at all. She'd just talked her way out of the home by making the doctor think they had.

And then there was this new lunacy about Peter.

I looked around the room at my family's expressions: Vanessa's eyes were again wide and round with disbelief. Dad was angry: he didn't like Peter. Jay didn't have an opinion one way or another, and Treavor was of two minds. He was obviously thrilled that he was gonna get Sue off his hands so easily. But on the other hand, he couldn't believe that she was telling him that she was leaving without even looking him in the eye.

"So you're going to go live at the beach with Peter?" I reiterated.

Again she grinned. "Yeah. The beach. With my brother." She noticed my disbelief and adopted fake seriousness. I could tell it was fake, because her eyes still twinkled. "I know you don't want to ever talk to him again, Bonnie."

Never. Why should I?

"But I'm here to tell you, you were wrong about him. He wasn't cheating on you with some random woman. All the evidence you found. . . It was circumstantial." A giggle broke free, and Sue covered her mouth like a school girl. She looked pointedly at Jay, and it was clear what she was trying to communicate: *I'm sure Peter wasn't cheating on you, but I'm just as sure that he most definitely is.*

Same old bullshit. Susan wasn't cured. Not in the least. The only thing that the doctors had changed was now she was giggling about her delusions instead of being angry and homicidal about them. She still believed Jay was cheating on me, only now it was funny to her.

But I imagined that this kind of crazy could switch back to dangerous in an eye blink. I shared a glance with Treavor, let him know we were simpatico on the relief thing. I was glad to get rid of my sister as much as he was, glad she was leaving town. I was thankful she would be away from Jay.

But moving to the beach with Peter? Where the hell had that idea come from? It seemed so entirely unlikely, but on the other hand, who was I to look too closely at the teeth on this gift horse? As long as Susan was going, I didn't care who was taking her.

But . . . Peter? When had Peter ever cared about Susan's wellbeing? When had he ever cared about his sister at all? In all the time that we were together, I don't think I could recall his having mentioned her once. And she'd lived on the other side of a closet from him then. Now he was probably living large at the beach, persona non grata, incommunicado, all those words that meant *not welcome, not around,* and it was obvious that was the way he liked it.

"I just wanted to warn you that he's on his way," Susan was telling me, "so you don't have to run into him if you don't want to. I'm just gonna pack a couple suitcases for tonight, but I'll be back for the rest of my stuff soon. And my car. Peter'll bring me back to get it. I . . . I just want to be going right now."

She leaned over and patted her wordless mother on the shoulder. "Now you guy's'll finally have the place all to yourselves!"

Susan looked around the table once more, again, smiling and making eye contact with everyone but Treavor. "I wanna say, thanks again for all your love and support, and again, I'm sorry I flipped out a little bit. I'll sure I'll be seeing you all soon!"

Her enthusiasm was still in total opposition to her words. It was like hearing someone speaking in baby talk, then realizing they were cussing. It was completely bizarre. Susan was so totally not cured! If anything, I thought maybe she seemed a little worse. She'd never been one to be walking around with this kind of a big smile. Maybe it was the meds. Or maybe she was having fresh delusions, of God-could-only-imagine-what, that were making her smile.

She skipped out of the room and up the stairs to pack.

We all looked at each other in amazed silence for a second, then Jay clapped his hands, making us jump, which had been his intention. "Well," he said to Treavor, "I guess that's the name of that tune, my friend."

"Thank Christ," my Dad murmured. "You've dodged a bullet today, son."

Vanessa frowned at him, then again arose and quickly went out into the kitchen. She didn't want to talk to any of us. She was embarrassed by her daughter's . . . *illness,* her utter lack of a decent apology for what she'd done.

"Let's get out of here before she changes her mind," Jay said.

He didn't have to tell Treavor twice. He stood up, said goodbye to my Dad, reached across the table and shook his hand, turned and was out of the dining room and then out the door before I'd taken two more breaths.

"I'm gonna stay and help her pack," I told Jay. He came around the table and hugged me. "I'll be home in a little while."

He said okay, and also shook Dad's hand. Then he was gone, and Dad went to out to the kitchen to comfort Vanessa, so I climbed up the stairs to help Susan.

The truth is, I was curious about this totally out of a clear blue sky offer from Peter. I wanted to hear all about that.

Sue was throwing clothes into two suitcases, open on the bed, humming to herself, as befitted someone newly released from the mental hospital.

"When did you talk to Peter?" I asked.

"Yesterday. He came to see me . . . So today I talked them into letting me come home. It took all damn day. First, I had to talk to the counselor, then Dr. Crowell, then some fat woman I'd never seen before. I thought, *Who the hell are you to shrink me, Shamu? You can't even push away from the table!*"

Sue grinned, and I knew there was some of the old her left. The crazy hadn't totally taken over. She's always had this kind of a mean streak.

"But I convinced her, too."

Susan looked down at her suitcases. She had packed them quite haphazardly, various clothes and unrelated toiletries, a wire hanger, a broken cell phone charger, half hanging out all over the edges. Her suitcases suddenly made me think of the lifeboats from the Titanic: half empty, not at all being utilized to their full potential. Sue swept the stuff inside and snapped them closed anyway, then looked at me, trying to be serious. But her eyes danced merrily, like a lunatic, and her smile was too big.

"I wanna say I'm sorry again, Bonnie. And tell Jay I'm sorry."

It was amazing, it was disconcerting. It was downright scary. She wasn't sorry at all.

"I'm sure I'll be seeing you soon." Susan gave me a clumsy hug, and her communication through that was just as transparent as her tone. She didn't want to see me ever again.

Dad and Vanessa were scarce when Sue came downstairs, but she didn't even look around for them to say goodbye. She didn't care about them, either. She was so *very, entirely* glad to get away from all of us.

Susan picked up her purse from the dining room table, and took her suitcases out on the porch. She hadn't said another word to me, so I figured our goodbyes had been said. I didn't follow her outside.

I watched through the window as she set her suitcases down right next to the street, and sat herself upon the bigger one, to wait for Peter. She took out her phone.

That was an hour and a half ago.

154

Vanessa and Dad also peeped out at her a few times, but she hasn't turned and looked at the house once. I've just been standing behind the door and watching her through the window, and typing all this on my phone. Susan's been busy looking down at her own phone all this time, so maybe that explains why she hasn't come back in, why Peter hasn't shown up yet. I'm sure she's in contact with him, and I'm sure he's explained why he's late. Killer traffic from the beach, perhaps.

I'm still gazing out the window at her – Vanessa's just walked away again, shaking her head – and another thought's struck me. I know my eyebrows went up, and I imagine I have a rather comical expression of surprise on my face. Because, after all, Susan, my beloved sister, has just been released from the mental hospital, where she landed because she tried to kill my wonderful boyfriend, because she'd imagined cruel, awful things about him, someone who wouldn't in a million lifetimes even dream of doing the things she'd accused him of doing.

And it occurs to me – maybe she's imagining all this, too.

Maybe Peter's not coming.

****